GHOSTBOY
AND · THE ·
MOONBALM
TREASURE

GHOSTBOY
AND · THE · MOONBALM TREASURE

BY RICHARD HAMILTON

illustrated by SAM HEARN

BLOOMSBURY
CHILDREN'S
BOOKS

First published in Great Britain in 2006 by Bloomsbury Publishing Plc,
36 Soho Square, London, W1D 3QY

A CIP catalogue record of this book is available from the British Library

ISBN 978 0 7475 8266 3

Printed and bound in Great Britain by Clays Ltd, St Ives Plc

5 7 9 10 8 6 4

All papers used by Bloomsbury Publishing are natural, recyclable products
made from wood grown in well-managed forests. The manufacturing processes
conform to the environmental regulations of the country of origin.

www.bloomsbury.com/childrens

For John Rolt – R.H.

For Aunt Bet and Uncle Pete and
the lunchtime chinwagging – S.H.

Chapter 1

The clocks struck twelve, midnight. As moonlight fell upon the ancient stones of Halibut Hall, two ghostly figures scurried across a courtyard and up a flight of steps. They moved silently, and so lightly that they almost seemed to be floating. One of the figures was tall and stooped, dressed in a long black coat and tails; the other was a boy in baggy shorts and boots with no socks. They were the butler and the kitchen boy of the house. They were both dead. They had been dead for a hundred and fifty years.

The door creaked as the two spirits entered the house. An owl hooted. They tiptoed down a passage, past the stern faces in the portraits on the wall, through shafts of cold moonlight that cut through the arched windows, and stopped in front of a door.

'This is it,' whispered the tall ghost, the butler. He rubbed his hands together and cracked his fingers.

The boy ghost read the words 'Indian Room' in gold lettering on the door.

The butler tried the handle.

'It's locked,' he whispered. 'You first.'

'No. You first,' The boy folded his arms. 'It was your idea.'

The butler made a little humming noise and tugged his ear nervously.

'Are you frightened?' asked the boy.

'Don't be ridiculous,' snorted the butler pulling himself together. '*I'm* the frightening one!' He rolled his red-rimmed eyes and smiled with a row of half rotten teeth. 'Haaahaaaaaa-huuuuuuuuurhhuuuuuurrrr-uurrrr-hurr,' he laughed softly and evilly.

'Crikey, Grandpa – you'll scare her to death,' grinned the boy.

'That would be nice,' smiled the butler. He drew himself up to his full height and coughed – ahem!

– before stepping straight through the closed door. The boy took a deep breath and followed, shuddering as he went.

'Alexander! You're on my toe!' hissed the butler.

'Sorry, Grandpa,' the boy apologised.

They stood still, blinking in the darkness. Portraits of Indian maharajas loomed over them. Huge ivory elephants stood either side of the fireplace, caught in a pool of moonlight, with rubies for eyes. From a large four-poster bed came the sound of deep contented breathing.

'That's her,' whispered the butler. 'A guest of Lady Halibut, down for the weekend. She is a computer scientist or something. I overheard her tell His Lordship there was no such thing as ghosts!'

'What? No such thing as ghosts?' the boy said in mock horror. 'We shall have to show her the error of her thoughts, eh Grandpa?'

'Alexander,' whispered the butler, winding a loose thread from his coat round and round his finger.

'Yes?'

'I don't know – I don't know if I can do it.'

'Of course you can, Grandpa. I know you can.'

'But . . . she was so very stern. Look at her – she is like a dragon, Alexander.' The butler leaned over the sleeping woman and eyed her quivering nostrils.

'And you are a dragon-slayer, Grandpa! Go on — put out her fire, give her a spine-chiller! Make her hair stand on end! Please, Grandpa.'

The butler sniffed, wiggled his wing collar and brushed down his black coat and tails.

'Very well,' he replied. 'I shall try.'

He stalked around the bed, looking like a hungry heron. Then suddenly he reared up and loomed over the sleeping woman. Gradually he grew brighter and brighter. A cold green light spread through his body, flickering gently, lighting up the exotic carvings of elephants and tigers and snakes that wound around the four posts of the bed. In a few moments, and with a great effort, the butler was shining. Now he was visible to humans. His eyes were wide. His hair was wild. Very slowly, he began to hover in the air.

The boy stood behind him, much dimmer, too dim for humans to see. He crossed his fingers.

'Whhhooooo,' the butler sang.

'Whhhooooo,' echoed the boy.

'We are the ghosts of Halibut Hall!' sang the butler in a reedy voice. He flapped his arms up and down.

'More light,' urged the boy.

'I can't,' hissed Grandpa, 'I haven't got it in me.'

'Halibut Hall, Halibut Hall,' echoed the boy eerily.

'Whhooooooooeeee.'

The boy frowned. His grandpa sounded as if he were a neighbour calling 'Cooeee!' across the fence. This was not good. This was not frightening.

The butler blew in the woman's ear.

He tweaked a toe sticking out from under the duvet.

He dropped a cobweb on her lips.

'Whhooooooooeeee.'

'The ghosts of Halibut Hall are here.'

'Halibut Hall, Halibut Hall,' echoed the boy.

The woman began snoring.

Grandpa paused. His hands on his hips.

'The ghosts – WAKE UP!' he shouted, losing patience.

The woman's eyes sprang open and stared at the butler. She had a strong face with a firm square jaw and coils of tousled hair. She looked in astonishment at the butler. For a moment fear flickered across her face.

Grandpa grinned, showing off his half-rotten teeth. Alex watched. This was the bit he liked.

'Boo!' said Grandpa playfully fluttering his eyelids. Then he rolled his eyes, theatrically.

The woman's lip trembled. She swallowed and blinked. Then suddenly she sat up and screamed: 'GO AWAY, YOU HORRIBLE OLD MAN!'

Grandpa shot up in the air and briefly passed through the top beam of the four-poster bed. 'Ow!' he cried as a curtain flopped down into him and he fell back on to the bed.

The woman narrowed her eyes and grabbed a pillow, which she held in front of her as if for protection. 'I don't know who you are – but if you are as you appear – a rather moth-eaten butler – then . . . Get me a gin and tonic!' she demanded as if she were the Queen of England. 'And don't take all night about it.'

Grandpa's jaw fell. His glow lost its brightness and he flickered weakly like a dying light bulb. 'But–but–but,' he began crawling off the bed, straightening his hair and smoothing down his coat. 'Yes, madam,' he said in confusion.

'Go on Grandpa – turn her blood cold. Turn her hair white!' cried the boy dancing around.

The butler looked at his grandson, desperately. He turned to the woman and began to chant in a small, uncertain voice:

'Beware the horrible Halibut curse,

The curse of Halibut Hall–

On October the third at half past five–'

'Oh, do be quiet,' snapped the woman, 'and don't

give me any more of this haunty nonsense, please,' she told him, abruptly.

'Oh!' The butler stopped. He coughed apologetically. 'No, madam. Certainly not, madam. Certainly not.' He began backing towards the door: 'I suppose you weren't just a little bit frightened? Madam? Just for a second? Eh?' He looked at the woman hopefully, blinking his bloodshot eyes and wringing his hands.

'No. Of course not,' she replied. And snorted like a racehorse.

'Ooooooooooooooooooohh!'

wept the butler as his light fizzled out and he fled from the room, his wailing dying away down the passage.

The boy Alex stood by the fireplace, too dim for the woman to see. How dare she upset his grandpa! He was almost hot with anger. Before he left he picked up the woman's clothes on the chair and threw them all out of the open window.

'Rotten ghost,' spluttered the woman throwing back the covers and getting out.

Alex stuck out his tongue: 'Bllleeeeeeeeaaaaaaar!' And he ran.

Chapter 2

Alex swirled through the corridors of Halibut Hall, searching for Grandpa. It was terribly dark but he knew every tuft of carpet, every knot in the floorboards. He passed a couple of suits of armour, more portraits of eminent Halibuts from long ago, and the hideous stuffed hippo head.

He found Grandpa in the attic room, beneath the sloping roof. He was sitting on his bed with his head in his hands and a cup of cold tea on the bedside table.

'Boo,' said Alex softly.

'Ah, boo,' replied Grandpa sadly.

'Come on Grandpa – it's not that bad,' Alex sat

next to him. 'That woman was a tough one. She wouldn't be frightened by the ghost of Genghis Khan!'

'It's no fun being a ghost any more,' complained Grandpa. 'Humans are just not frightened. They couldn't care less. What's the point in being a ghost if you don't frighten anyone?'

'Some humans are frightened,' Alex told him.

'Not of me. Not like they used to be,' Grandpa sipped his tea. 'How long have we been ghosts?'

'A hundred and fifty years,' replied Alex.

'A hundred and fifty years,' repeated Grandpa. 'Ever since we were suffocated in smoke − here in the attic − you and I have been haunting Halibut Hall. We have frightened Lord Halibuts and Lady Halibuts and dozens of Little Halibuts. But − Alexander − the time has come to face facts. I am losing my touch.'

'No, Grandpa. You're just tired. Appearing before humans is very tiring. It takes all your energy.' Alex put his hand on Grandpa's shoulder. 'You're just as frightening as you always were. Remember the opera singer who screamed so loudly the windows in the west wing shattered?'

'Yes − but that was fifty years ago. Just now that

woman in the Indian room ordered a gin and tonic! I'm not a butler – I'm the *ghost* of a butler. I don't serve spirits – I *am* a spirit!'

Alex managed to smile. At least Grandpa still had his sense of humour.

'I know – let's cover ourselves in blood and appear – that'll give her a shock.'

Grandpa shook his head wearily.

'Or, or – I know! We could give her a gin and tonic with an eyeball floating in it!'

Grandpa attempted a little smile. 'Nice – but – I think I'm going to bed,' he said, ruffling his grandson's hair affectionately. 'I'm awfully tired.'

Alex wandered along the passages of Halibut Hall kicking his heels. There was nothing to do. He crept into Lady Halibut's room and tied a few knots in her hair. He undid some threads on His Lordship's trousers, so that the buttons would pop off and the trousers might fall down. He found a dead fly and dropped it into the cook's bedside water. He hid a house guest's underpants up the chimney. He didn't go back to the Indian room. He didn't want to meet that woman again.

Instead he went downstairs, past the suit of armour and Lord Halibut's arrangement of antique swords and spears. It was all very well being a ghost, he thought, able to wander around frightening people, able to walk through doors and walls (though that was uncomfortable and sometimes painful); and it was fun to fly along corridors, going 'Whhhhhoooooooooooooooooooo!' – but after you had done it for one hundred and fifty years, it was ... well ... a bit *boring*.

He wandered through the dark ballroom to the even darker library.

He had a date with Sir Henry Halibut, Elizabethan sea captain. Sir Henry was a marble statue.

'Good evening, Sir Henry. How are you tonight?'
The statue was silent. Not a whisker stirred.

'I'm bored,' said Alex as if in answer to Sir Henry's greetings. 'Tonight's apparition went badly. The human was not frightened by Grandpa. Not at all. And now Grandpa is upset. I hate to say it but . . .' He whispered in Sir Henry's ear, '*Grandpa is losing his touch.*'

Sir Henry didn't move.

'I love him dearly, of course,' Alex continued, 'but we've been together in this house for a hundred and fifty years – we've never gone anywhere and there's nothing more to talk about. Since we've been ghosts, we've talked about the invention of the telephone, the photograph, the car, the aeroplane, the atomic bomb, the computer. We've talked endlessly about the harvest, the weather, the birds, cloud formations. Grandpa likes to talk about cloud formations: cirrus clouds, cumulus clouds, mackerel skies. Every day, every week, every year. For a hundred and fifty years. It's driving me mad. It's *boring* me mad!'

Sir Henry was silent. He was made of marble. He was bored solid.

Alex slumped in the chair by the window.

He fished out a penny from one of his pockets which bulged with useful things, and began to toss it over and over. Heads. Tails. Heads. Heads. Tails.

He stood up and took a tour of the library. Some papers left by Lord Halibut on the round table rustled as he passed, and he blew them on to the floor watching them see-saw gently through the air. An old globe spun as he pushed it with his finger. He closed his eyes and stabbed at the globe to stop it spinning. He peered to see where his finger had landed. Greenland. He wondered what Greenland was like, but couldn't find the urge to look it up in one of the books that lined the walls. He left the library and went to the kitchen looking for some mice to frighten.

Rooting around in his pockets he found his one hundred and fifty-one-year-old conker on a string. It was as hard as iron. He twirled it around his finger. Banged it against a saucepan. Bong! He wished Grandpa played conkers.

Why was Grandpa losing his touch?

It couldn't be the food, as they'd been eating the same things for a hundred and fifty years and anyway what they did eat (and that was hardly anything) they couldn't taste.

It couldn't be an illness because as far as he knew, ghosts didn't get ill. (Well that made sense – they were already dead, weren't they?)

Maybe he was upset by the new motorway that had been built twenty years ago? Or the planes. Grandpa hated the planes. They'd been waking him up for at least forty years.

Alex sat in the rocking chair by the range and looked out to the parkland.

If only ghosts could benefit from the planes or the cars, he thought. Humans were lucky, they got to use all these fantastic inventions – while he and Grandpa could only listen to the noise they made.

He envied humans. They were so . . . alive. They could taste and smell and touch everything. Oh, so many things, so many wonderful things. Food and flowers and freshly mown grass. Ghosts could see and hear all right, but everything else was turned off. It was only a half-life. Like living underwater. It was like trying to find a bar of soap in the bathwater – you caught it and then it slipped away. You caught a smell or a taste – but only for a moment – and then it was gone.

Maybe it was something to do with appearing before humans. He could always smell more things when he appeared. But a ghost could only appear before humans once in a while, because it was so tiring ... the rest of the time they were just too dim to be seen by humans.

What was that?

As he was thinking, Alex saw something moving outside in the parkland. His heart jumped.

It was someone walking up the drive towards the house. A tall, white figure. A tall, white, *ghostly* figure.

Alex stood up. He jammed the conker in his pocket, along with the coins and stones and other useful things.

This was new. This was *something happening*. At last! He wanted to jump up and down with excitement. Their first visitor for ages. At least five years!

Chapter 3

F.A.O
Mr Trethowen
Halibut Hall

URGENT.
BY HAND ONLY

B.G.H. LTD

The ghostly visitor moved purposefully through the parkland. Her faint light shimmered as she passed under the old oak trees. The sheep backed away, somehow wary of her presence. Alex went to the hall window to get a better view. It was a woman, a grown-up. (It was always a grown-up – why could it never, ever be another child ghost?) She was a modern ghost: funky flat cap, big collar and flares. Very 20th Century. 1970s, Alex guessed. She walked straight up to the front door and looked around. Spotting Alex through the window, she waved. Then, smiling, she walked slowly and deliberately through the big oak doors that were bolted shut for the night.

'Ooooh,' she shivered. 'Hello.'

Alex almost swooned. She was fresh and relaxed and happy. A fashionable modern ghost! She smiled at him – she positively beamed at him. No one had ever smiled so broadly.

'Hello,' he managed to say.

'Gosh! You live in the middle of nowhere!' she exclaimed. She had enormous eyes, like a beautiful deer.

Alex couldn't help grinning foolishly. 'Do we?'

'The place that time forgot!' laughed the woman pushing her cap back a little.

'Oh, that's me – us – we're late for everything,' Alex boasted, laughing even more foolishly and wondering what he was talking about.

The woman put a hand in the satchel she was carrying and pulled out an envelope.

'I'm Julie from B.G. Holidays. Is Mr Trethowen here?' she asked. Her teeth were very perfect, very modern.

'Yes. He's asleep upstairs. Shall I fetch him?'

'No need,' came a weary voice. 'I'm coming. I'm coming.' Grandpa came down the stairs slowly, looking even more tired than before his sleep.

'Hi, Mr Trethowen! I'm Julie from B.G. Holidays!' the woman squealed. 'I've come with some fantastic news!'

'Really?' said Grandpa uncertainly.

'Oh, yes! Really. I think you're going to ... *explode* with happiness!' She beamed.

Alex felt like jumping for joy.

'Am I?' said Grandpa, looking faintly alarmed.

'You've won a holiday!'

Alex waited for Grandpa to explode.

'Goodness,' said Grandpa.

Alex waited for the explosion. Was that it? *Goodness*? Come on Grandpa – the woman was expecting more than that! Look – even now her smile was faltering ... They might take the holiday away if the winner wasn't more enthusiastic!

'YEEEEEEEESSSSSS!'

Alex whooped joyfully. He seized the Big African Spear from Lord Halibut's wall of weaponry and threw it headlong at the suit of armour on the stairs.

YEEESSSSSS!

There was a tremendous clatter. The armour fell over in pieces and the head bounced down six stairs, and lay spinning on the floor like a disembodied hip-hop dancer. The spear lay embedded in the wood panelling.

Julie looked horrified.

Grandpa clapped his hands to his ears. 'Alexander,' he spluttered. 'Lord Halibut is asleep upstairs!'

Alex realised his explosion of happiness was bigger than strictly necessary. 'Sorry,' he whispered.

They stood listening, looking up at the ceiling. Grandpa's lips pursed. 'His Lordship will be down in four minutes, precisely. Clear it up immediately,' he told Alex sternly.

Alex began to put the armour back together, at the same time listening to every word Julie from B.G. Holidays said.

'I'll be quick,' she told Grandpa with brisk enthusiasm and a flash of a smile. 'The details are all in the letter. You'll stay in a gorgeous five-star hotel, with all the latest luxuries: swimming pool, mud baths, light treatments, entertainers, lovely dank cellars, mournful music.' She giggled. 'All completely free of charge, for one week. We've arranged for a local carriage firm to pick you up tomorrow night: Castor Carriages? Are you familiar with them?'

Grandpa shook his head. He looked mystified, his mouth opening and closing like an old carp.

'I'm sure they're very good,' Julie beamed. 'When did you last have a holiday?'

'Oh, well, actually . . . I've never had a holiday,' Grandpa admitted uncomfortably. Julie made him feel as if he should have had one.

'Wow!' Julie raised both eyebrows and put her hand to her mouth. 'You must be dead tired. You'll have a fantastic time. It's so refreshing!' she giggled.

'Really?' said Grandpa. They heard a creaking floorboard above them.

'Better go,' Julie twittered. 'Have a lovely holiday.' She stepped away, took a breath and passed back through the front doors, waving as she went.

'How –' began Grandpa.

But she had gone.

'How did you get my name?' he said staring at the letter in his hand. 'How did I win? What . . . what do you do on a holiday?'

They opened the letter when they were back in the attic; while His Lordship was prowling downstairs in his pyjamas, muttering.

Congratulations! the letter said, in the same over-excited manner that Julie had used. *Following your purchase of Clammy Cold Teabags from Spectral Products Ltd, you were entered into the Big Ghost Holiday draw. And you have won:*

1st Prize!!!!!!!!!

'Oh, happiness!' Alex jumped so high that his head and shoulders disappeared through the ceiling for a moment.

'Ow,' he complained as he re-emerged into the room, holding his head.

'Hummm. Teabags?' Grandpa was sounding mystified. He read on.

All you need to do is to pack your things and be ready on Tuesday 25th June at midnight. You will be picked up by your local carriage – Castor Carriages – who will convey you to the unique and wonderful Moonbalm Hotel, Dr Jempson's famous hotel for ghosts! Compliments of the Big Ghost Holiday Company. You may bring one family member.

Then he read, in the voice of someone giving a graveside address: *Fancy a cuppa? Get the cool brew: Clammy Cold Teabags!* 'They never used to have competitions,' he muttered.

Alex fought to control his glee. He knew from experience that he mustn't try to force Grandpa to do something. But his toes were curling with excitement inside his hobnail boots.

'A holiday,' Grandpa mused. He was baffled. 'I've never had one. I wonder . . .'

'I've never had one either,' broke in Alex. 'But it would be so fun. I've heard about holidays. I've read about them. Loads of ghosts have them. Can we go? *Please* can we go? *Please.*'

'Stay . . . cool,' said Grandpa, stiffly borrowing a twentieth century phrase. He wiggled his wing collar. A smile played on his lips. He chuckled and then amazingly – he laughed. It was like rainfall after a drought. Alex realised then that Grandpa hadn't laughed properly for years. He had only ever performed his awful frightening, haunting laugh. This one was lighter, happier, more . . . tinkly.

'Better pack our bags,' he said and winked at Alex.

Chapter 4

Castor Carriages came early. Grandpa and Alex were packed and standing under the portico of Halibut Hall, ready to go. Each carried a small leather suitcase, containing a book and their wash things. Being ghosts, they only had one set of clothes.

The white carriage and two ghostly horses arrived suddenly. One moment all was still and silent, the next there was a cloud of dust and a snorting and stamping of hooves.

'Whoa!' cried the ghostly coachman, a dark shadow high up on the driver's seat.

Castor – None Faster! read the racy black letters across the carriage.

'Wow,' breathed Alex hopping up and down in his excitement.

'Ahem,' coughed Grandpa snatching his much-used handkerchief from his top pocket and covering his mouth and nose.

The coachman also coughed in the dust and jumped down. He wore a black hooded cloak and carried a long whip. He swaggered over to them and introduced himself.

'Castor from Castor Carriages. You'll be Trethowen,' he said, nodding to Grandpa. He turned his black eyes on to Alex and scratched the rough stubble on his chin. 'Who are you?'

'This is my grandson,' said Grandpa putting a protective arm around Alex.

The coachman twirled his whip, and cracked it dramatically. Then he made his eyes go very big. 'Jump in, then. And be quick: this carriage is an express.'

He wasn't a ghost to argue with, or pass the time of day with. They picked up their bags and climbed in.

'How far –' began Grandpa pleasantly.

'YA – HA!' cried the coachman, and the horses reared up. Half a second later the carriage bolted forward sending the two passengers sprawling on to the back seat.

'Hang on!' cried Grandpa. 'Wait.'

Alex hung on, but the coachman wasn't waiting.

'YA – HA!' he yelled again and cracked his whip, not once but three times. Now they charged down the drive. It seemed that every journey was a personal test for him: just how fast could he go?

Bouncing around inside the carriage, Grandpa scrabbled to the window and was about to stick his head out, when a pillar from the entrance to Halibut Hall swished by.

'Madman!' he squeaked.

Now the horses were galloping. Sparks flew from their hooves. The carriage lurched forward and back as it thundered through the moonlit countryside. Inside it felt as if a small earthquake was taking place. Even their voices were jolted by the shaking.

'I wish he'd t–t–t–t–t–take it e–e–e–e–e–easy,' complained Grandpa, trying to brace himself against the bumps.

'H-h-h-h-how long is the j-j-j-j-j-journey?' asked Alex.

'I don't – don't – don't – don't know,' replied Grandpa.

'I think I feel s-s-s-sick,' said Alex.

'Don't you d-d-d-d-dare d-do it here!' cried Grandpa.

An hour passed. Talking was impossible. Alex looked out of the window. Trees, fields, roads, fences, houses, lights all passed in a blur.

Two hours passed. Eyes shut tight, they clung on grimly.

Three hours passed. They were in dense dark woodland, bouncing around the carriage like loose sacks of potatoes. Every pothole made them groan. Every swerve made them slide along the seat and bash themselves on the side. They had headaches and bottom–aches.

'If only someone had invented seatbelts,' wept Grandpa.

'Or c-c-c-c-cushions,' moaned Alex, jiggling like a puppet.

At this point in their journey Castor the coachman had a problem: he was charging full tilt at a corner. Horses galloping, wheels spinning, dust billowing in clouds behind them. The problem was – did the corner turn left or right? There were no streetlights and he couldn't tell.

Ahead there was just a bank of trees. No signpost, no glimpse of the road past the bend . . .

He could slow down?

'Faster!' he roared, to banish that last cowardly thought.

Left or right?

Or stop?

Suddenly he pulled hard, pulled firmly, pulled with decisiveness.

To the right.

'If only –' began Grandpa, for the hundredth time. 'AHHH!'

The carriage veered decisively to the right at the exact moment the road turned sharply . . . to the left. Carriage and road parted company with a tremendous bump. For two seconds the carriage was in mid-air.

'Ohhhh!' cried Alex and Grandpa.

'Enough!' screamed Grandpa. His thin face and staring eyes appeared for a moment in the window of the carriage, before disappearing again as there was a second devastating bump that sent his head crashing through the roof.

Moments later the carriage smashed through a wall and came to a halt in a field of cows.

The horses stood panting in the moonlight.

'MOOOOOOO!' The cows ran to the other end of the field and stood in a pack gazing at the ghostly horses.

Grandpa stumbled out of the carriage into the field, rubbing his head. He had turned green – like the inside of a cucumber. Alex fell out of the door clutching his stomach.

'You raving lunatic!' Grandpa gasped. 'You speed-mad maniac!'

He looked around, still stamping his feet.

Castor, the daredevil coachman, had gone. His seat was empty.

'I *hate* going through walls,' complained Alex. 'It really *hurts* when you're not expecting it.'

'Where is he?' demanded Grandpa.

Back in the trees, Castor was dangling from a branch.

'Left,' he said kicking himself. 'I meant left.'

Chapter 5

An hour later the horses trotted smartly up the road and came to a halt in front of a sign. Grandpa was driving the carriage. Castor was sitting inside, under his hood there was a bandage around his head. He was injured and unhappy. Alex stood at the rear admiring the view. As far as he was concerned, the holiday was going splendidly.

'Look!' he cried as they came to the sign. He read it aloud:

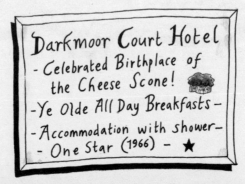

Darkmoor Court Hotel
- Celebrated Birthplace of the Cheese Scone!
- Ye Olde All Day Breakfasts -
- Accommodation with shower -
- One Star (1966) - ★

'This isn't it,' he said. 'The letter said nothing about cheese scones and all day breakfasts.'

'Calm yourself,' said Grandpa studying the map. 'That must be the sign for the humans. I am sure this is the right place. Look: what's that?' He pointed up the drive; there was a hint of excitement in his voice.

Alex saw coloured lights dancing in the trees. 'There!' he cried. 'Moonbalm Hall.'

Grandpa walked the horses forward through the gates to an avenue of chestnut trees. The multicoloured signs blinked at them and moved eerily around the trees. They read:

'Yippee!' cried Alex.

Around this swirled other flashing signs:

STRICTLY NO GHOULISH BEHAVIOUR

MOONBATHING

HUMOROUS HAUNTINGS PERMITTED

SLIME BEDS

WEAR HEADS!

Top Entertainment by DEAD FAMOUS™

COLD POND TREATMENT

'Oh, excellent,' Grandpa grinned and rubbed his hands. 'This *is* a holiday. I was beginning to think we would never get here.'

Alex smiled. He hadn't seen Grandpa so excited about something for — what? — a hundred years? More probably.

Grandpa shook the reins and the carriage wheeled round a dried-up fountain and entered the final length of drive that led to an imposing Victorian Gothic mansion. Alex looked about. The gardens were overgrown and unkempt. Rhododendrons spilled over the tarmac drive that was already full of weeds and potholes. It was a far cry from the manicured parkland of Halibut Hall — but then maybe that was because it was run by ghosts. Alex wondered how it managed to be a hotel for humans too . . .

The closer they came to the entrance, the shabbier it appeared. There was a leaking drainpipe that left a long green stain on the stone; there were four cars and a rusty minibus parked on the gravel drive, and a crumbling portico, under which stood a skeleton.

The doorman.

Grandpa made the brief but traditional fuss required upon arrival. 'Whoa! Whoa there! Good boys! Well done! Well done indeed!'

The skeleton danced forward and opened the carriage door.

'Thank you kindly,' said Castor, hopping out.

'Ahem,' said Grandpa who as a butler for sixty years could convey a variety of meanings with a simple cough. Sometimes it meant, 'Hello, I'm in the room', at others it meant, 'Don't you dare do that!' and again at others his cough could mean, 'Another potato, please'. In this case it meant, 'Excuse me – though it may look as if I am the coachman – I am, in fact, the passenger.'

The skeleton looked at him.

Skeletons aren't very bright, so this one just thought he had heard a cough.

'Sssssstep this way,' it hissed at Castor.

'This ruffian is the coachman,' interrupted Grandpa clambering down, 'who on account of a small accident has ended up in the carriage while I have become the driver.'

'Ssssso . . .' faltered the skeleton.

'So I am the guest, and I have won the Big Ghost Holiday Draw!' he boasted.

'Ooooooh,' said the skeleton pushing Castor aside rudely and turning to Grandpa. 'Ssssstep this way.'

'Goodbye,' said Grandpa to the coachman and handed him the whip. Castor hobbled over to the driver's seat and began hopping up the ladder.

'I'll be in the stables,' he told them. 'Recuperating.'

'Are you sure you should be . . .' began Grandpa.

'YA-HA!' Castor shouted, and he was gone, leaving everyone covered in dust.

'Bagssssssssssss?' asked another smaller skeleton in a breathy voice.

Grandpa dropped his bag on the gravel. 'Yes,' he said with pleasure, and watched as the skeleton picked up the bag and jangled off into the hotel.

Grandpa winked at Alex. 'This is the life,' he purred. Being a butler, he was one of the few people who could truly appreciate good service.

Chapter 6

Alex and his grandpa followed the skeleton under the crumbling portico and into the entrance hall of Moonbalm Hotel. Alex gasped — he had never seen so many ghosts before.

Opposite the long reception desk was a bench with a line of ghostly miners, all reading sheets of music, and humming tunefully. They had blackened faces and lamps on their helmets that lit up the music.

Beyond them, Alex could see the first tier of a splendid staircase. Ghosts were milling around the chairs and low tables at the bottom; a group of ladies in huge crinoline dresses sat talking by the fireplace; a large important-looking man in a frock coat and towering wig marched up and down chuckling with a thin man in a modern suit. Three dandies in doublet and hose seemed to be comparing their elaborate footwear.

Grandpa stepped up to the desk. Immediately a ghost materialised through the office door. He wore a long purple robe covered in intricate gold embroidery and a vast white turban that towered above his head like a cloud. He had a deep, sonorous voice.

'Welcome to Moonbalm Hall, Mr Trethowen. Where Ghosts Go to Get Away. Huuu-uuuu-haaaa.

We've been expecting you. I am Dr Jempson, at your service.' He bowed and his eyes swept across them, stopping abruptly at Alex.

'Who's this?' he asked as if a nasty smell had just wafted past his nose.

'My grandson,' said Grandpa.

Dr Jempson's eyes emptied of warmth and welcome. He spoke in a whisper. 'Children are not allowed in this hotel.'

'Well, I didn't think . . . Look – my letter clearly states that –' Grandpa fished out the Big Ghost Holiday letter and handed it over.

Dr Jempson scanned it. He tutted several times and rearranged his turban.

'No one informed me,' he complained and stamped his foot. For a moment he looked quite angry and then he closed his eyes and breathed swiftly, deeply in. When his eyes opened, he was calm again. 'Your boy can stay with you in . . . Room 27. Raleigh will show you. Sunrise today is at 4.58 a.m. so we would request that you be in your quarters by that time. Dinner at 3.30 a.m. Before that, there's a quiz in the library: "Famous last words and hilarious headstones" – it's fiendishly popular. I've seen a great deal of swotting going on – and there's a prize: fresh flowers delivered to your grave every month for a year!'

'What if you don't have a grave?' asked Alex.

Dr Jempson frowned. 'Choose someone else's. They may have the flowers,' he snapped.

'Oh, don't worry – we have headstones,' said Grandpa trying to keep things light. 'Hard to read, now, of course, covered in lichen and whatnot.'

'Bird poo,' added Alex cheekily.

The doctor leaned over Alex and fixed him with his powerful stare. 'Children are not allowed in the library, the billiard room, the games room, the swimming pool, the mud room or the music room. I'm sure you understand.' He paused. 'Raleigh,' he called softly and put out his hand to ring the bell.

Ding!

Alex's mouth opened to protest. He wasn't allowed . . . where? This was a holiday! He glanced at Grandpa. Grandpa gestured to him to keep quiet.

'Quite so,' the butler said eagerly to Dr Jempson. 'We do understand.'

A skeleton swung over and nudged Alex rudely out of the way.

'Yeeessssssssssssss?' it said.

'Take Mr Trethowen and his grandson to Room 27, please. Enjoy your stay.' Dr Jempson smiled and vanished through the closed office door.

Room 27 was on the second floor, in the attic of the main house. They passed up the grand staircase under a dome flecked with peeling paint, then up another back staircase to the attic. On the way they passed various signs written in light:

On some doors Alexander noticed a red cross.

'What are the red crosses for?' he asked.

'Occupied,' hissed the skeleton. 'Humansssssssss! Huh.' he said, showing his disgust.

Well, we all were once, thought Alex.

'Don't go in there,' warned the skeleton, his teeth snapping. 'Dr Jempson don't like it.'

' "Dr Jempson don't like it",' mimicked Alex behind the skeleton's back.

'We'll be at home up here, won't we?' said Grandpa cheerily, as they reached the attic area and found Room 27, high up under the eaves with a view past the decorative battlements out to the front.

'Enjoy your sssssssssstay,' hissed the skeleton and departed into thin air like steam from a kettle.

Chapter 7

'**B**ut I'm a hundred and fifty-nine,' objected Alex once the skeleton had left and they could talk properly. 'I don't see why I should be forbidden to go anywhere.'

His grandpa sighed. 'As I have explained a trillion times, when you departed the mortal life, in the smoke-filled attic of Halibut Hall, you were nine years old. I was sixty-nine. And so, as ghosts, we will remain for ever – nine and sixty-nine.'

Alex bit his tongue. He didn't want to have this discussion for the trillion and first time. He didn't want to ruin the holiday for Grandpa. (Especially now that he was looking so happy again). His feelings towards Dr Jempson were another matter. He decided he must stay out of his way.

'So I shall allow you full run of the hotel – except those places restricted to grown-ups – and you can explore the grounds as much as you wish. However, you must respect the other guests and stay out of mischief.'

'Yes, Grandpa,' said Alex, obediently. Standing on his bed he found that he could look over the battlements to the front of the hotel and see the drive and the grounds bathed in moonlight. He realised it would be quite easy to climb out on to the roof.

'It is such a relief not to have to do any haunting tonight,' said Grandpa peering into the small bathroom that had been clumsily built into a corner of the room. He glimpsed himself in the mirror.

'Ahhh!' He laughed merrily. 'I frightened myself! Ha ha!'

'You don't have to be frightening here,' Alex reminded him.

'No, indeed. I will be charming. My kind and cuddly side will come out. Now – I am going downstairs to have a little look around before dinner. Will you come or shall we meet in an hour in the dining room?'

'I'll meet you in the dining room,' Alex replied, finding himself slightly disturbed by the thought of Grandpa's kind and cuddly side. He thought Grandpa was rather stiff and cold. Like a butler ought to be.

'Very well.'

Alex waited until the door closed and Grandpa was gone.

Phew!

He threw himself on to his bed. And almost immediately sat up again. He had an hour to look around Moonbalm Hall. He must explore every inch. It was a shame that there wasn't another child ghost, especially as there were so many other ghosts. Still, he was used to being on his own. And there might be one somewhere – hiding in the pipes or in the stables or something. Maybe he could play some tricks on Dr Jempson? Muddle up the room keys or drop spiders in his turban? No, he'd have to think of something better.

He put his bag on the bed by the window and left the attic room, running along the dark passage and taking the first staircase he came to.

The staircase spiralled down to another floor. He went through some doors with a notice that read: 'Fire doors – keep closed' (he nodded with approval at that). The stairs ended in a long corridor. It was dark and empty. It was a more modern wing of the house, not at all Victorian Gothic . . . more like a shed with windows. Moonlight filtered under numbered doors that ran along one side.

At the end there were more fire doors and more stairs that led down to a large empty room with a wooden dance floor and a bar covered in tinsel. 'Disco Bar', a notice said. No disco dancing tonight. The room was deserted.

However the swimming pool, just outside the Disco Bar, was in full swing. Alex saw a dozen ghosts lying on chaises longues, moonbathing. Several ghosts were on lilos, bobbing about in the water, sipping cocktails. It was particularly odd as they were fully clothed. One ghost in a tropical safari suit was paddling an inflatable canoe. Another, in an overcoat, was reading a book. The water didn't seem to bother the ghosts. On the poolside a skeleton stood with towels hanging on his arms, and an assortment of snacks ingeniously tucked between his ribs.

Alex felt a pang of sadness that he wasn't allowed to go into the swimming pool. But he shrugged it off and carried on exploring.

He opened a small door near the Disco Bar. It was a broom cupboard. He tried another: it was full of bottles and cans of drink. He left the bar and went along the ground floor of the modern wing, past some dried-up plants to another door. Here he found steps leading down.

He took them and was immediately back in the old part of the house. There were cobwebs and old junk and stacked firewood in one area, and rusty bicycles and washing machines in another. He crept through a series of different little rooms, all dark and damp and unused by humans. As he passed by a pile of old paint pots he noticed a faint white light a little way off. He tiptoed quietly towards it.

In the gentle glow of a candle, four ghosts were bobbling around in baths while two skeletons hovered nearby. The ghosts were playing cards on a table in the middle. The baths, Alex realised with disgust, were full of pondweed and slime. Slimebaths! The ghosts looked like gangsters – they wore vests and had cigars stuck in their mouths, and stripy suits and panama hats hung on hooks nearby.

He tiptoed past and went up some stairs emerging in the main part of the hotel. He peeped into a room called 'East' and saw some old ghosts – *ancient* wrinkly ghosts – in leather armchairs. They were all asleep with their noses pushed into books or newspapers. He stared for a moment, tempted to play a joke – maybe drop some soap into that open mouth or tie that ghost's necktie to the plant behind him . . .

In another room (called 'South') there were six ghosts having a dancing lesson. He left them and went along a corridor, past the Snug Bar (full of laughter) and a tearoom (full of muttering) to the reception hall. The miners had gone and Dr Jempson was busy attending to a newly arrived fisherman who'd drowned in his nets as Alex scurried past avoiding Jempson's eye, and ran swiftly up the main staircase.

At the top, on the square landing under the dome, Alex saw again the rooms with red crosses on the doors – the humans' rooms. Despite the skeleton's warning, he wanted to see inside. So when no one was looking, he slipped through the closed doors.

In each of the first two rooms he found one human asleep. They both looked solid and firm and fleshy. Their business suits lay nearby. Out of habit he hid their socks under the carpet.

The third room contained a pair of messy humans, snoring loudly and surrounded by half-empty takeaway Chinese meals. He found a prawn from one of the meals and popped it between the toe of one of the sleepers, sniggering as he did so. The men had walking boots and maps and elaborate equipment with wires. They also had a garden spade. It bothered Alex. Why would anyone come to a hotel and bring a garden spade?

There was only one other room with a red cross on the door. It was a dormitory room with beds down each side, full of huge hairy men and piles of sports equipment. He examined their bags. He guessed they were a Russian ice hockey team. He did so want to tweak their moustaches or tickle their toes or push spiders up their nostrils – but he resisted the temptation.

Back on the landing, in an alcove off the main staircase, he found a laundry chute. It was like a slide. Alex opened the doors and climbed in. Then he slid straight down to the cellar and landed in a big basket! Fantastic! He spent a minute or two jumping about in the sheets and pillow cases. Then he lay back. He wished he could share this with someone.

But there was no one. It was the same as ever.

He climbed out of the laundry and pushed open a door nearby. He was outside now in a cool, overgrown garden. He breathed in the sweet summer air. If he were a human, the taste and smell of that air would surely be heavenly.

He walked across a lawn, springy with moss and riddled with molehills, to some steps. The steps were long and wide with weeds growing through the cracks. He sat down in the moonlight and gazed at the urns and balustrades hidden under ivy. He looked at the moon shadows. He admired a statue of a huge warrior about to throw a spear. He could see how this was once a grand garden. But what a dreadful, run down state it was in now!

And if there was no one to play with, where was the fun? He hoped he'd find someone.

'WHO ARE YOU?' demanded a voice.

Alex looked around. He couldn't see anyone. But you never knew with ghosts. Some of them could change into any shape they wished.

'Alex,' he called out.

'You're a boy. Boys are not allowed in the hotel,' said the voice.

That made Alex prickle with anger. Why couldn't boys be in the hotel? What was wrong with boys? He stood up and addressed the air. 'Why not?' he asked. 'That's a stupid rule. And I think that you are a coward for not showing yourself.'

'COWARD?' barked the voice with an odd squeak at the end.

At that second Alex realised to whom he was talking. It was the statue. Except it wasn't a statue. It was a ghost warrior. A huge one. He met the warrior's eyes, alive with indignation and his heart jumped. The warrior's spear was pointing directly at him. Suddenly it was flying through the air. There was a whoosh as it flew past Alex's ear.

'Hey! I'm sorry. I didn't see you,' cried Alex holding up his hands in surrender. 'I thought you were hiding. I didn't mean to call you a coward.'

In one leap the warrior was next to him. Alex saw long wild hair, blue warpaint, fierce eyes framed by an iron helmet.

He also realised it was a woman.

'Hotel security,' she said picking him up by the shirt with one hand. 'Who are you?'

'Alex Trethowen.' He swallowed nervously. 'I'm staying here. With my grandpa. Room 27.' Alex's legs dangled in the air.

The warrior dropped him. 'No one told me,' she said grumpily. Her anger seemed to deflate like air escaping from a balloon. 'I'm always the last to know.'

She strode over to the wall and plucked her spear out of the stone. 'When he changes the rules, he should have a staff meeting. Call us all together and tell us. Otherwise I could go around ejecting guests willy-nilly.'

She regarded Alex for a moment. Alex thought she was magnificent. A warrior queen.

'Haven't seen a boy for ages,' she said cocking her head and gazing at him as if he were a peculiarity. 'Sorry about the spear – bit of an overreaction, but I do like to throw it. I'm Etheldread. I work for Dr Jempson. Have done for ages. You could say I've been in "security" since the Dark Ages.'

'The Dark Ages? Are you from the Dark Ages?' asked Alex, who had never met a ghost this old.

'No – I'm not from the Dark Ages – I'm older,' Etheldread told him, fierce and proud. She struck a pose. 'I'm from the tribe Iceni. We fought the Romans, two thousand years ago. I'm buried over there.' She pointed out to the woods. When she looked back at him, her face softened. 'You must come and see my tomb some time. It is a place of wonder – or so I'm told.'

'Yes, I'd like that,' said Alex.

In the distance they heard the *bong! bong! bong!* of a dinner gong.

'You'd better go,' Etheldread told him, kindly now. She reached out her big hand and touched Alex on the cheek. 'Little scamp.'

Chapter 8

There was a queue of about a hundred ghosts all lined up to go into the dining hall. It was one of the strangest sights Alex had ever seen. They were of different sizes and from different times, dressed in the fashions of their day, according to their position in life. They all seemed very lively and jolly. There were lords and ladies standing next to fishwives. There were soldiers and millers. There were hanged men and drowned women. There was a wrestler and a Viking, a wizard and a clown with enormous feet. There was even the ghost of a dog.

But there were no ghost children. Except him.

'Ah, there you are,' said Grandpa, calling above the

hubbub. 'This is my new acquaintance: Miss Mary Gibbons from Marfleet in Hampshire. This is my grandson, Alexander.'

Grandpa was bubbling with excitement – Alex could hardly believe the change that had come over him. He seemed to be bursting with energy.

'How do you do?' said Miss Gibbons, speaking in a light little voice and blinking behind her gold glasses. She wore a long, early Victorian dress with fancy lace cuffs and a high collar.

'Hello,' said Alex politely.

'And this is my other new acquaintance: Crinkle the Clown.' Grandpa winked. He thought Crinkle would be a great companion for Alex. Crinkle had a mop of hair, big baggy trousers and ridiculous outsized feet. He smiled at Alex, then slowly produced a pink paper flower from behind his ear and handed it to him.

'Thanks,' said Alex. He held it awkwardly, wondering how he would get rid of it politely.

Crinkle became preoccupied with his feet. They were a metre long and got in the way. Unsure where to put them, he pointed one shoe out of each side of the queue.

Alex listened to their conversation, quietly stuffing the flower into his already full pocket.

'And how are you finding the food?' Grandpa was asking Miss Gibbons. 'I gather it is rather good here.'

'Oh, it is good,' she replied. 'I could definitely taste something yesterday.'

'Me too!' said Crinkle in a high voice. 'I had a banger and suddenly I remembered – you know, the smell, the sizzling, the juiciness, the . . . the pure *porkiness* of a sausage. Just for a second. I had a glimpse of heaven,' he swooned.

'Stop it. Please,' said Grandpa, his mouth watering. 'Don't torment me. I've tasted nothing since I died.'

'Poor you. But it is normal,' said Miss Gibbons consolingly. 'Oh! To taste and smell and touch and feel again,' she lamented. 'To march across the moors with rain dashing upon your cheeks; to eat strawberries in some honeysuckle heaven, to run my hands through softest rabbit fur . . .' The others looked at her in surprise.

'Was you a poet?' interrupted Crinkle.

'Oh, yes,' Miss Gibbons admitted bashfully. 'Well, I dabbled.'

'Marvellous,' said Grandpa admiringly. 'To be a ghost and have words to remember things by. Even if we cannot taste and smell, with the right words we can imagine and get close, don't you think?'

'Oh, yes,' said Miss Gibbons nodding earnestly and blinking behind her spectacles.

The doors opened and they all filed into the dining room and took a seat at one of the long tables. Alex sat down next to Grandpa and turned to see who was sitting next to him. He started.

It was a bearded man in chain mail with an arrow sticking out of his eye.

'Hello,' Alex said shyly as the man caught his look and stared back with his good eye. 'Are you . . . are you . . .'

'Am I King Harold who got one in the eye at the Battle of Hastings? No! I am not,' said the man touchily. 'There's plenty people got arrows in the eye in my day. And other places.'

'Sorry,' said Alex. 'I didn't know.'

The man across the table – who looked like a cowman with his curious floppy brown hat and white smock – leaned over to Alex. 'Ever seen Pete the Pike? 'Ee got a pike in the belly, run right through! Everywhere 'ee goes 'ee got a eight-foot pole poking out. Har! Folks do laugh!'

Alex grinned back. There were some oddballs here, that was for sure. Nothing normal about ghosts.

At the end of the hall the skeletons had gathered. They were holding platters of food and now began to serve the ghosts their meal.

There was no choice tonight. Fish and potatoes. Strawberries and cream. Both were served at once with little ceremony. The ghosts sniffed the food hopefully and ate it. It was completely tasteless. Strawberries tasted like fish, fish like strawberries. Both like nothing. They might as well have served them on the same plate.

'I had hoped,' said Grandpa, 'that I'd taste *something*.'

'Imagine,' said Miss Gibbons, trying to conjure up sensation, 'the crunchy batter, the firm white flesh, tangy with the sea – then the ripe fresh sweetness of the strawberry and the glorious thick whipped cream . . .' She positively gurgled with pleasure.

'Ummmmm,' Grandpa closed his eyes. He took a mouthful. Chewed. 'Nothing,' he said disappointed.

'Might as well serve cowpats,' said the cowman earthily.

Alex laughed. He stopped himself when he saw Miss Gibbons' disapproving looks.

The meal finished and the skeletons cleared the plates away. They were about to get up when suddenly silence fell. It was as if someone had switched on the lights. The ghosts stopped talking. They stopped moving. They stood or sat stock still as if they were caught in the middle of a game of musical statues.

In fact, someone *had* switched on the lights.

It was a human. A young woman in a dressing gown. She had a mug of tea in her hand and was walking through the ghosts to the French windows at the end of the hall. The ghosts parted to make way for her. They made not a sound. The young woman, the human, simply couldn't see them.

She put her tea on Alex's table. Miss Gibbons stood up quietly, moving carefully out of the way, watching all the time. The woman opened the shutters to look out of the window, and stood there, surrounded by ghosts. The sky was lightening in the east, very faintly. She sat down and took a sip of the hot tea.

'Ahhhhhhh,' she breathed with relief and closed her eyes. Then she opened them and looked around, as if puzzled by something.

Alex stared. He glanced at the other ghosts – some were licking their lips. Some just let their tongues hang out. Were they remembering what it was like to taste hot sweet tea?

'Oh, for a cup of tea,' whispered the cowman, his eyes watering.

'And the feel of a soft dressing gown,' said Crinkle.

'She looks unhappy,' Grandpa said.

'She must be in love,' said Miss Gibbons softly.

At this the ghosts around them seemed to swoon a little. They sighed all together.

'Remember love?' said Grandpa wistfully.

They watched the human in silence, remembering their own lives.

'Pssst.' The cowman nudged Miss Gibbons.

Suddenly they realised that the dining room was emptying. Dr Jempson was floating towards them gesturing them to leave. 'Leave. Leave immediately!' he hissed flapping his arms like a big purple bird.

And they moved towards the door, caught in his hypnotic stare.

He didn't like ghosts getting too close to humans.

The ghosts went to bed. They fled up the stairs, floating, running, swirling like mist over the red carpet and round the pillars and balustrades. It was time. Day was coming. Alex and Grandpa followed. All over the hotel, doors opened and shut, silently.

Grandpa lay on his bed and fell asleep immediately. But Alex wasn't tired. He looked out over the battlements to the dawn just coming up.

It was all very well having a rule for the grown-up ghosts – but child ghosts had more energy. They could easily stay up during the day. It was exactly the other way round from humans. Adult humans stayed up while their children slept. Alex didn't see why he had to go to bed if he wasn't sleepy – or who would stop him if he did stay up.

He saw the sun rise. He heard the birds sing. He thought what a wonderful hotel it was, how there was still so much more to discover. He was about to climb into bed when he heard a chugging noise.

He looked over the parapet and saw a large bus coming slowly down the drive.

It was old, a single-decker, with red and cream lettering on the side and a throaty engine noise. The driver was an old lady. She eased it into a parking space, scrunching over the gravel, and stopped with a 'ttsssccch' of the air brakes.

Humans. Now it was human time again. The coach was empty apart from the driver and one passenger.

Out of the side of the coach stepped a slender girl. A child. The old lady followed, she was tall and stately and had a walking stick.

Alex looked at the girl and smiled. She might be a human, but she was *his age*.

He tiptoed to the bathroom and picked up a little bar of hotel soap from the basin. Then he went back to the window and as the two humans passed under the entrance he threw the soap over the parapet.

Chapter 9

Missed! Alex watched the soap sail through the air, just clearing the bush that grew out of the crumbling portico, but landing well behind the two humans who had just arrived. Boohoo! He could see its little blue shape lying in the gravel.

But a moment later the girl returned and stooped to pick up the soap. She looked at it suspiciously. She looked up at the hotel then back at the soap in her hand. You could see her thinking: *Who threw that?*

'It's raining soap!' laughed Alex.

He felt suddenly very mischievous and decided to sneak downstairs. As it was daytime the ghosts would all be asleep and he could have some fun with the humans. He'd just have to make sure he didn't bump into Dr Jempson.

He whispered 'Boo,' to Grandpa, (noticing how his mouth now turned up at the corners as if he were having a pleasant dream) and he sneaked out of Room 27. He wondered what the girl was like. He hoped she wasn't someone easily frightened. He wanted to play jokes on her, not frighten her. He hoped she was the sort of girl who liked to climb trees, and have imaginary conversations and play imaginary games. Just to watch her would be fun for him. He shut the door quietly then swooped through the corridors and slid down the banisters by the grand staircase all the way to the ground floor. He popped his head into Dr Jempson's office. It was empty.

In reception, the girl and the old lady were waiting. Alex prowled around, wondering which trick he could play. The bags? The keys? The light switch? He started by moving one of the flowers in the flower arrangement on the counter. Just a little. The old lady didn't notice, but the girl did. She began watching the flower. It was a lily and Alex made it swivel its head as if it were reading the sign next to it. ('Please deposit your keys at reception before leaving the hotel'). The girl frowned. She couldn't believe what she was seeing.

Suddenly the flower sneezed.

'Atchoo!'

'Bless you!' said a young woman popping up from behind the counter. Alex jumped: he had had no idea she was there.

The lady and the girl looked at each other. 'Wasn't me,' said the lady.

'The flower –' began the girl, then thought better of it.

'Mrs Crump?' inquired the receptionist.

Alex recognised the receptionist: she was the same young woman who had been drinking tea in the dining room earlier.

'Yes, that's me. And this is my granddaughter Claire,' the lady told her. 'We've booked a couple of nights.'

'That's right. I have your details here,' the young woman began studying the papers.

'Sorry to turn up in the coach, but we've just taken a group of Japanese tourists up to the Lake District and we're on our way back.'

'That's fine – there's plenty of parking,' said the receptionist. Alex jumped up and sat on the counter watching the exchange.

As they spoke, two men came down the stairs. They were wearing outdoor clothes, waistcoats with dozens of zip pockets, hats, small rucksacks and sturdy shoes. Alex recognised them. They were the ones with the Chinese meals in their room.

'Excuse me,' the smaller man interrupted. 'Have you got our order for packed lunches?' He zipped and unzipped one of his pockets.

'Of course.' The receptionist began looking for a list.

'Disorganised as usual,' muttered the man rudely. His eyes were close together and he had a thin sneering mouth.

Mrs Crump glanced at him, clearly irritated that he should interrupt like this. Her granddaughter was watching him too. He drummed his fingers on the counter and tutted. He rolled his eyes at his tall companion. The earflaps of his hat twitched oddly.

'I'm sorry, I don't seem to . . .' began the receptionist.

'Oh, that's all right – I'm beginning to get used to it at this hotel,' said the man in a mocking tone.

Mrs Crump and her granddaughter stood patiently. The man's left earflap rose in the air. It looked very odd. It had a grey woolly underside. He looked like a vintage car indicating a left turn.

'Are you going for a walk?' asked Mrs Crump trying not to stare at the earflap.

'We had hoped to have a stroll before breakfast, but I doubt if there'll be time at this rate,' replied the man, unpleasantly. Now his right earflap began to move up and down. Flap. Flap. He frowned.

'What are you grinning at?' he asked the girl called Claire.

'Nothing,' she said flushing.

The man glanced behind him.

'Ha ha! How do you do that?' asked Mrs Crump with a little laugh.

'Do what?' asked the man, his earflaps now flapping furiously.

'Hey! Ha ha! Your hat!' his tall companion snorted with laughter. 'You're like an elephant! You'll take orf soon! Ha ha. Oi!' he exclaimed as his own hat was suddenly jammed down over his eyes.

'You stupid buffoon,' snapped the short man. He grabbed his earflaps and held them down. 'We'll take our walk now – just make sure the lunches are ready to collect after breakfast,' he ordered the receptionist and strode out of the entrance, followed by the tall, gangly man.

Mrs Crump lifted a quizzical eyebrow.

The receptionist shook her head.

'You wouldn't believe it, but their names are Sweet and Sour,' she confided. 'The tall one is Mr Sweet; and the little one – well Sour by name, sour by nature . . . a real sourpuss! They've been here two weeks – making a map or something.'

'If you want my opinion,' said Mrs Crump, 'they are extremely rude and unlikeable. I hope their packed lunches give them tummy aches.'

With that, Claire and her granny took their key and went to their room. Soon afterwards they came down to breakfast. Sweet and Sour were already there – without their hats – and so was a man in a suit.

As they sat down there was a cry from Mr Sour: 'Look out, you oaf!' It seemed the sugar bowl had been mistakenly tipped over.

Moments later Mr Sweet pushed his finger deep in the jam. 'Really – I didn't mean to – it just did it,' he apologised, spreading the dripping jam on to his toast with his finger.

Claire leaned forward to her Granny. 'They're weird!' she said.

'They certainly are,' agreed Granny. 'We shall steer clear of them, shan't we?'

When breakfast came, they were amazed at the size of it. 'When they say "All Day Breakfasts", do they mean it will take you all day to eat?' asked Claire.

Her granny laughed. She was a big woman, but her granddaughter was small and had the appetite of a bird. She watched Claire hesitate when trying to put a forkful of sausage into her mouth.

'What's the matter?' Granny asked. 'Not organic?'

Claire's mouth was open to receive the sausage, but the fork wouldn't go near her mouth.

'It's . . . it's like someone's holding it . . .' said Claire as the fork waved around in front of her. Suddenly the fork flicked upwards and the sausage flew off and hit Granny in the eye.

'Claire!' Granny scolded and wiped her eye with her napkin. 'Don't play with your food.'

'Sorry – I didn't mean to,' Claire was bewildered.

But then Granny's fork began to behave strangely.

It began jabbing itself around the plate. Granny held it as it speared a whole sausage, a fried egg, three mushrooms and a baby tomato and hovered in the air in front of her mouth.

'I don't want all that!' gasped Granny staring at her fork in disbelief. She held on to the fork and fought to get it back on the plate. But it came towards her mouth, quivering. Granny opened wide, and slowly, carefully, the fork manoeuvred its way into her mouth, filling it entirely.

'Granny!' Claire exclaimed in awe.

'Ummm-ummmm-ummm,' replied Granny.

Claire looked away. And that's when she suddenly glimpsed a little boy sitting beside them, laughing. He was dressed in a white collarless shirt and grey shorts with bulging pockets and boots with no socks and his hair was sticking up . . .

He turned to her and his laughter froze. His mouth fell open.

'Granny – who's that?' whispered Claire. She nodded in the direction of the boy – and realised he had vanished.

Vanished! That was exactly the word, because there was nowhere for him to go, no time for him to hide. Yet he had gone.

'Oh!' Granny swallowed and gasped. 'My fork has a mind of its own! I would never, ever try to eat such a gargantuan mouthful. I do beg your pardon.' Then she burped – something Granny *never* did.

'A thousand apologies,' she said, wiping her mouth.

'That's OK, Granny.'

'I shall have awful indigestion, stuffing myself like that.' Her eyes watered.

'Did you see the boy?' Claire asked.

'No,' said Granny, still recovering.

Claire looked back at the space Alex had occupied.

I've just seen a ghost, she thought calmly.

At that moment there was a loud crash from the direction of Sweet and Sour's table. It seemed that they had finished their breakfast, but when they got up to go, they had both fallen over and sent the table crashing to the floor.

'Some blinking idiot has tied our shoelaces together!' Mr Sour spluttered at the astonished diners.

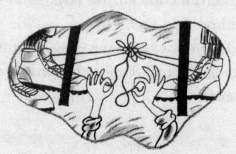

Chapter 10

Alex left the dining room in happy confusion. He had enjoyed playing pranks on those humans, especially the men, most especially the small rude one.

But the girl, Claire. Something had happened then, something that confused and unnerved him. He was sure she had seen him – *without him showing himself* – something that had never happened before.

He walked into the garden, thinking.

Usually a ghost had to *try* to appear. You had to make an apparition – an appearance – and show yourself, as Grandpa had done to the woman in the Indian room. But it took enormous energy and often you couldn't appear again for several nights. But the important thing was that Alex hadn't tried to appear, the girl had just seen him.

And that could mean only one thing.

It meant that the girl, Claire, was a medium – a human who could see and talk to ghosts, without the ghost going to the trouble of appearing itself. It was a gift. There were very, very few of them. Sometimes they didn't even know that they were mediums. Claire didn't know she was a medium – Alex felt sure of that – because she had looked as surprised as he had been.

He wandered in the gardens, still thinking. He passed arches and grottoes hidden behind overgrown bushes. He found an orangery, with broken windows and twisting vines by the edge of the woods.

The woods led down to a river that snaked slowly through the valley. Alex discovered a little boathouse and sat on the jetty watching the river glide past. He wished there was a river at Halibut Hall. He could spend weeks gazing into the swirling currents.

If the girl was a medium, would she be able to see other ghosts, he wondered? Or was she just tuned in to see him? Some instinct told him to be careful. He wondered if he could find a book in the library that had information on mediums. He might even visit tonight . . .

He dangled his boots in the water, watching the water pass through them. It gave him a funny tingly feeling in his feet. He watched the clouds reflected in the water moving against the current across the eddies and swirls . . .

Suddenly a huge helmeted figure burst out of the water in front of him.

Etheldread!

'Bah!' she exclaimed, shaking her armour.

The water came up to her waist, swirled through her.

'Hotel security!' Etheldread announced, then seeing it was Alex, she softened her voice. 'Oh. It's you. What are you doing out of bed?' She sounded disappointed.

'I couldn't sleep,' Alex told her.

Etheldread shook her head. Her braids swung either side of her heavy iron helmet. 'That's why we don't have children at the hotel,' she grumbled. 'They're always bored. They never sleep. They've got too much energy. Hey – do you want to see something special?'

'OK,' said Alex.

She scooped him up in her powerful arms and waded to the bank. Then continued effortlessly into the woods, stopping in front of a steep cliff that rose from its base by the river, up into the woods.

'Would you like to see where I live?' she asked putting him down.

'Your tomb? Oh yes!' Alex had never seen an ancient Briton's tomb before.

'I'll hold your hand as I go in,' Etheldread said,

'otherwise you'll never find it.'

She grasped him firmly and then walked to a particular spot that was covered in ivy, and then she went straight into the cliff face. Etheldread pulled Alex after her.

Suddenly they were in darkness, in a cave cut into the rock, sealed by a stone door in the cliff. The curved stone walls loomed in the greenish light of the two ghosts.

Alex shuddered. Going through the rock was cold and uncomfortable. The cave itself was dry but chilly.

'My tomb,' Etheldread announced in the darkness. Her voice echoed. 'Sealed for two thousand years. Come on.'

Alex walked forward, tentatively, his eyes slowly growing accustomed to the dim light after the bright daylight outside. He saw the rough walls, saw swords and spears and shields lying lined up. At the end of the cave there was a raised area where a great cask lay, surrounded by chests of treasure. Alex whistled. Goblets and jugs and jewellery and gold plates glinted in their ghostly light.

'That's something isn't it?' said Etheldread proudly. 'We got that from the Romans, when we smashed their camp at Sowchester.'

'This has been here for two thousand years?' Alex picked up a goblet and admired it.

'Almost. I died saving my queen,' Etheldread told him proudly. 'She hid these things with me after the battle. To thank me.'

'They're amazingly shiny.'

'Of course! I polish them,' Etheldread held up a big round platter. It was smooth, and they could see themselves in it. Big ghost of ancient Britain and little ghost of Victorian kitchen boy.

'Is this where you live? I mean, do you sleep here?' Alex shivered.

'Every afternoon. Me and my supplies.'
Etheldread opened a chest and took out some old
biscuits and a gold jug. She put the biscuits on the
cask and filled the jug from a little trickle of water
that sprang out of the rock. Then she took out
some silver plates and goblets. She arranged them (a
little fussily) on the top of the cask. She motioned
Alex to sit on a stone ledge.

'Tuck in,' she said. 'Eat as much as you like.'

Alex took a biscuit. He guessed this was ancient
Britain's version of tea with Granny.

'At least it's a nice big coffin,' he said.

'Ummm,' Etheldread agreed with her mouth full.
'It's mine.' It was funny to think of her bones in
there.

'It makes a good table,' said Alex. He was thankful
the biscuit was tasteless. It must be centuries old.

'Made to last,' said Etheldread. They both chewed
hard.

'Did you kill a lot of Romans?' Alex asked when
he finally managed to swallow.

'Dozens!' Etheldread chuckled. 'I met one later –
about a hundred years ago. He came to the hotel.
A foot soldier from Gaul. He was a nice ghost.
We greeted each other like old friends. He showed

me his wound: very nasty, in the leg. I showed him my treasure. He was very impressed. He said it was good enough for an emperor. In fact, he was pretty sure that most of it once belonged to an emperor.'

There was something straight and uncomplicated about Etheldread. Alex liked her. He felt she was loyal and trustworthy. So he asked the question he was longing to ask: 'Etheldread, have you ever met a medium?'

'A human who can talk to ghosts?'

'And see them too. See ghosts, without the ghosts having to try.'

'No. Never,' Etheldread replied. 'They are very rare. If you ever meet one then you are lucky. The first ghost they see is very special. They say it brings the ghost closer to the living. But Dr Jempson doesn't like them. He says they cause trouble, because they see ghosts all the time and they go poking their noses into ghost business.'

'What would you do if you met one?'

'Me? Well, I suppose I'd talk to it and see if it was friendly.'

Etheldread sneaked a look at the boy, but didn't ask anything more. She was someone who liked to keep their thoughts to themselves.

Chapter 11

The clocks struck twelve. Midnight. All through the hotel the ghosts stirred. They stretched and yawned, climbed out of bed and dressed. Some took just a couple of moments to dress – the poor or the modern who just had a few garments to throw on, maybe a T-shirt and shorts or a smock and pantaloons. Others had ball gowns and wigs, or doublet and hose, or battle armour. That was tiresome, especially when one was on holiday.

Alex's grandpa slept with his clothes under the mattress, in order to press them and keep them smart. Now he got them out and put them on. He smoothed out the creases as best he could. He spat on his shoes, then rubbed them clean and wiggled his wing collar. Ready for the night! He looked over to Alex's bed.

It was empty.

The butler pursed his lips. He hoped Alex was behaving.

The queue for breakfast stretched into the hotel reception and Grandpa scanned it, looking for Alex. He spotted Miss Gibbons.

'Good evening!' he said warmly. 'Did you sleep well?'

'I did indeed,' she said with a smile. 'I dreamed I was travelling on a donkey in Italy.'

'How lovely,' said Grandpa. 'For the whole night?'

'Oh, yes. It's a big country. I dream a little part of the journey every night. I'm in Umbria now. Just south of Assisi.'

'Marvellous,' said Grandpa. He had dreamed that he was laying the table for a splendid banquet, with seven courses and four different wines. 'You haven't seen my grandson Alexander, have you?'

'I'm afraid not.'

They watched as Crinkle the Clown came down the stairs in his big red shoes.

'Bad luck dying in those shoes,' muttered Grandpa.

Miss Gibbons laughed; a little tinkly laugh. And they all filed in for breakfast.

From the upstairs landing Alex watched them go in. After leaving Etheldread he had snatched a few hours sleep, then got up before Grandpa. He didn't want Grandpa to know what he was doing. He had decided to talk to the human girl, Claire. He needed to see if she was really a medium with the gift to see ghosts. And if she was, was he the first ghost she had seen?

When the ghosts had filed into breakfast, he went up to her room. It had one of Dr Jempson's red crosses on the outside to show it was occupied by humans. Alex ignored that and stepped through the door. He found the granny human fast asleep in the main room. In a room off the side, he found the girl, Claire. He quietly closed the door between the two rooms so as not to disturb the girl's granny. He tiptoed over to the bed.

The girl was also asleep, breathing deeply and evenly. She had mouse brown hair and long eyelashes and healthy red cheeks. She was a thin whisp of a thing, just like him. Alex searched her face for clues as to what sort of person she was. He'd looked upon thousands of sleeping faces. Sometimes you could tell a lot from a face. The furrowed brow of the worrier; the pursed lips of the sour; the laughter lines of a happy person. Claire's mouth lifted naturally into a smile and her hands were held together under her chin. He decided she was a cheerful person but a careful one. He guessed she was also determined. But brave? He'd find out.

Alex sat down by the bed. He made no effort to appear. If she was a medium, she would see him without him trying.

'Claire,' he whispered.

She stirred.

'Claire.'

She opened her eyes. Bleary at first, then suddenly alert. She looked directly at him. She *could* see him. She swallowed.

'Hello,' Alex spoke kindly. 'My name is Alex.'

Claire lay watching him. She heard his voice as if through water, far away, though he was only a few feet from her. She could feel her heart pumping blood. Thump thump thump.

She realised that she was looking at a ghost. A little ghostboy, with knobbly knees and a thin weaselly face. The more she looked the clearer he seemed to become. She should scream, scream like mad to send him away. She opened her mouth.

Nothing came out. Because she didn't scream. She wouldn't. Shaking, she edged away a little.

Claire wasn't going to be frightened by a ghost. If it really *was* a ghost. She wasn't that sort of girl.

After all, she told herself, *this is just a little boy. Boys aren't scary*. He was the boy she had seen this morning when they arrived. If he *was* a ghost, this may be her only chance to talk to one . . . She summoned her courage, and not caring that she felt a little foolish, whispered:

'Hello.'

So she is brave, thought Alex.

He smiled. A friendly, crooked smile. He rubbed his cheek and then leaned forward.

'Did you see me this morning?' he asked. He spoke more clearly now. He hadn't moved but somehow he felt closer.

Claire nodded. 'Yes. I did.' She studied his clothes – he looked poor. He wore no socks in his clumpy boots and his shirt was thin and threadbare. She kept her eyes on him. She didn't *think* he was dangerous.

'I'm a ghost,' he told her.

Claire swallowed. Although she knew this instinctively, it was good to hear it from him. 'How do I know you're a ghost?'

The boy stood up and walked towards Claire. He kept on walking into the bed, through the bed to the other side. 'Can a human do that?' he asked.

'No way.' Claire sat up, her amazement suddenly overcoming her fear. She was fully awake now. 'What does it feel like?'

'Horrible,' said Alex pulling a face. 'It jangles all your nerves. It makes you feel shaky.'

'Who are you?' Claire asked.

'I'm Alex Trethowen, the kitchen boy at Halibut Hall. I died a hundred and fifty years ago in a fire at the hall – well, actually me and my grandpa were suffocated by the smoke in the attic. And that's where we haunt now. We're the ghosts of Halibut Hall. Whooooooo!' Alex rose in the air and flapped his arms. He wasn't trying to be frightening, and in fact the effect was rather comical.

'Can you do anything else?' Claire asked, her mind racing.

'I'm not a freak show,' Alex told her.

'No. But you are unusual. There are not many like you, are there?'

The boy smiled, as if this was a joke. If only she knew that there were indeed many like him.

'What do you want?' she asked suddenly.

Alex hesitated. 'Am I the first ghost you've ever seen?'

'Yes.' Claire said truthfully. 'You are.'

'Brilliant!' Alex smiled broadly. 'I thought I was – I mean when you saw me this morning, I almost fell over backwards. I'd done all these jokes . . .'

'That was you? At breakfast?' Now Claire understood. 'You made Granny eat that big mouthful?'

'Who did you think it was?' Alex laughed. Was she going to be angry with him? Oddly enough, he had never been held responsible for his jokes before.

'I wasn't sure,' she replied. 'Did you play jokes on those men? Sweet and Sour?'

'Yes, that was me.'

Now Claire smiled. 'It was funny. I don't like them.'

'Why not?'

'Well, they were quite rude to everybody. As if they were terribly important and nobody else was.'

'That's all right then?'

'Yes,' she said. She lay back in the bed and pulled the covers around her. For a ghost Alex didn't seem very spooky . . . 'Do you live here?' she asked.

'Oh, no. I'm on holiday here with my grandpa.'

'On holiday?' Claire laughed. 'A ghost on holiday! Whoever thought of —'

'Yes,' retorted Alex, stung. He had thought that she would be frightened of him, but she wasn't at all. 'Ghosts have holidays too, you know. It's not only you humans.'

'Where's your grandpa, then?' asked Claire.

'He's downstairs with the others. Having breakfast.'

Ghosts having breakfast! This was getting

ridiculous! Claire closed her eyes. She pinched herself. When she opened her eyes again, Alex was still there. Watching her. She felt a bit shaky. Should she hide under the covers and wait until he had gone? No, she decided. She should seize the opportunity. Be brave. When would she ever get the chance to see ghosts having breakfast again?

'OK,' she began climbing out of bed. 'You show me the ghosts having breakfast. If I see that, I'll believe you.'

'I don't know if you *will* be able to see them,' Alex said uncertainly, 'but I can show you where they are. Only you must stay hidden. If they see you, you might frighten them.'

'*Me* frighten *them*?' said Claire. That would be interesting. She hadn't brought a dressing gown so she put on her coat and pushed her feet into her trainers.

'Are *you* frightened of me?' she asked, standing up.

Alex looked at her in her pink spotted pyjamas and silvery green coat and trainers.

'Of course,' he said breaking into a smile. 'You're taller than me.'

They went down the back stairs, Alex leading the way. Claire made sure that he was always several steps ahead of her. She didn't want to get too close. She had so many mixed feelings. She wanted to touch him, but she didn't. She wanted to be brave, but she felt her bravery draining away. At the bottom of the stairs there was a door leading to the garden. He certainly knew his way around the hotel.

Alex opened the door and stopped.

'Get back,' he said suddenly.

Claire stepped away from the open door and looked past Alex to the garden. At the far side of the lawn a figure in a cloak – a *ghostly* figure – suddenly shot out of the bushes on a motorised lawnmower. He zigzagged madly across the lawn, then disappeared, bumping down some steps.

'What was that?' whispered Claire.

'That's Castor,' Alex explained. 'He's a coachman. He brought us here.'

He glanced at Claire. She looked alarmed, but said nothing.

'I think it's better if no one sees you,' Alex told her.

Claire agreed and, keeping close to the building,

they crept past the darkened windows until they came to the dining room. The windows ran from floor to ceiling and there were three of them. The first two had the curtains drawn and they couldn't see in. The last one had a gap. Very slowly they peered around the window frame through the gap in between the curtains.

'There,' said Alex.

Claire looked in. She held her breath.

'Oh my —'

A hundred or more ghosts were sitting down at breakfast, served by six skeletons. The ghosts came from every age, were dressed in every fashion, and had died in different ways. And some carried their way of dying with them, a wound or an illness, or an accident. A hunter half-eaten by a lion. A woman stung to death by bees. A man who had died in his sleep. (He was still in his pyjamas — in fact he looked as if he was still asleep.)

She was suddenly terrified. Fear welled up in her.

'So? Believe me now?' said Alex.

But Claire was already running back.

Chapter 12

Images of ghosts, weirdly white and transparent, crowded through Claire's mind as she ran back to the cellar door. Some of them were strangely dim, as if she hadn't been able to see them properly, but their presence, like bits of swirling mist, was undeniable. Others she had seen clearly: the soldier with his blasted tunic and expression of surprise frozen on his face; the prim schoolmistress in glasses, the funereal elegance of the Victorian butler.

'I shouldn't have done that. I shouldn't have shown you,' Alex admitted, catching up with her on the stairs. 'I'm sorry.'

Claire spun around. 'Stay away from me,' she hissed, holding up her hands. She didn't want to see any more ghosts now.

But Alex wouldn't go. He followed her as she stumbled up the stairs to the first floor.

'I'm sorry,' he pleaded. 'I mean you no harm. And nor do they – they are on holiday. They never haunt on holiday. It's safe, I promise you.' Alex was angry with himself. He should have taken it more slowly.

Claire ignored him. The ghostboy was behind her, following, but not too close. She wanted to wake Granny, she must wake Granny. She took the stairs two at a time and luckily at the top turned the right way down the short passage and found the door that led to the landing and then to their room.

She felt safer from the moment she was in the room. Granny was sleeping peacefully curled on her side away from the door. Claire hesitated. She imagined trying to explain to her . . . how stupid she would sound . . . how like a worried little girl, not the brave girl she wanted to be. She decided she must deal with this situation herself. She would not wake Granny. But the sight of Granny was good − it had given her strength.

She was aware too that the ghostboy had joined her in the room. He was watching her nervously.

Be brave, Claire told herself. She clenched her fists. She squeezed the cuff of her coat hard and walked briskly through to the small room off the side. There was her bed. She climbed in, kicking off her trainers but still wearing her coat. She pulled the covers over her head, and shut her eyes tight. She wanted to think. She concentrated on breathing steadily and evenly.

The hotel was *crawling* with ghosts. Weird and terrifying ghosts. That was why soap dropped from the sky and their food had a life of its own and people's shoelaces were inexplicably tied together. Why there were bumps and bangs and knocks in the pipes. And she was talking to one of them. He may not be frightening but the rest were.

Yet she would not run away. What did Granny say? She must be open to experiences. Say 'yes' to every experience. That was Granny's motto.

Claire peeped over the covers. The boy was still there. He looked quite small and harmless in his shorts and boots. He had such pale, pale skin, yet his face was quite alert and cheeky.

Now he was examining a chocolate bar that the hotel had left for the guests. He caught her looking.

'What does chocolate taste like?' he asked turning the bar over in his hand. 'I never had it. Not when I was alive. Some did, but I never did. Everyone eats it now, don't they?'

Claire nodded. 'It's sweet and... filling ...' she told him.

'Do you believe in me now?' The boy put the chocolate down and faced her.

'I think so, yes. I believe you exist. I believe you are on holiday.' The boy looked happier. 'But why me? Why do I see ghosts? Why did I see you at breakfast and no one else did?'

'It's because you are a medium,' Alex told her. 'Do you know what that is?'

Claire shook her head, wanting to hear what he thought it meant.

'It means you can see ghosts and talk to ghosts, without them having to try to appear. For most humans we have to perform an apparition – but you see us naturally. You can see both worlds. That is really unusual. It's a gift.'

Claire had never thought of herself as unusual. She wasn't even sure she wanted to be. Alex continued:

'And because you're unusual – that makes me unusual, because I found you first! Anyway, I'm on holiday and there's no one here of my age. In fact, there's no one my age at home either. You've no idea how *boring* it is being a ghost.'

Claire smiled. By chance she found her teddy under her pillow and she held his leg and listened to the boy ghost. He liked to talk. He began to tell her all about life at Halibut Hall. How he haunted it at night, how he lived with his grandpa and they had long ago run out of new things to say to each other, how tiresome it was not being able to taste or feel or smell properly. How they envied humans.

He didn't need much prompting, but when he did, Claire asked a question and Alex was off again. He talked and talked and paced up and down her room. Before they knew it, several hours had passed and Claire couldn't stop her eyes fluttering shut. Suddenly Alex realised she was asleep.

Chapter 13

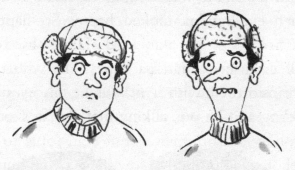

A lex left Claire with his ears ringing and his tongue strangely tired. He hadn't talked like that for years. He had a friend. A friend his age, who listened to him, who hadn't heard all his stories, who might play with him. A whole new landscape of possibilities and conversations and activities to fill in the endless ghost hours now opened up before him. And what's more, his friend was a human. That was a surprise. *Just wait till Grandpa hears,* Alex thought, *he'll have a coughing fit!*

He ran down the stairs, marched past the reception desk with a quick wave to Dr Jempson, (who scowled with suspicion – that boy was up to something) – and out into the moonlight. He was restless and the night was not yet over.

He saw Grandpa further off on a bench talking to Miss Gibbons. He was holding her hand. But Alex stopped – Grandpa looked happy. So happy in fact, that Alex felt unnerved. He realised he'd hardly ever seen Grandpa happy. His whole face was transformed with a new light, his eyes were twinkling and he was talking merrily. Alex smiled.

Grandpa had found a friend too.

Alex turned and walked away from them. He took some steps down to a square garden and ran along the weed filled paths. There was a warm wind on his face and clouds were scudding across the sky. Behind Alex, Moonbalm Hall seemed to rise and sink in the changing light, as the full moon appeared and disappeared behind the clouds.

He made his way to the abandoned orangery beyond the square garden and down the hill towards the edge of the woods. It was a little building just a bit bigger than a summer house and standing on its own, with a view across the valley. He went inside. There were windows from floor to ceiling, and vines growing over one end, filtering the moonlight and leaving leafy shadows that danced across the floors.

Chairs and tables were stacked up against the back wall. Alex perched himself on a table and thought how wonderful it was to talk to a human again. How beautiful it would be to be fully alive.

He heard a twig snap, and looked up. Outside he heard voices.

Humans?

In the middle of the night?

Out of the woods came Mr Sweet and Mr Sour. They carried bags over their shoulders. They looked heavy because the men grunted with effort as they moved them. Alex thought there was something suspicious in the way they kept looking around.

Sour pushed open the glass door. It scraped on the stone floor.

'This is good,' he whispered to Sweet, his voice echoing in the emptiness.

Picking his way carefully to the far end, through the moon shadows and the cobwebs and the dead leaves on the floor, Sour looked around. There was a slatted bench under the window where fingers of ivy had pushed their way through. Sour pushed the bag under the bench and studied it.

'That's all right for now,' he said turning to Sweet who was just coming in with three more bags.

'You're joking,' Sweet disagreed. 'Anyone can see it.'

'No one comes here,' said Sour curtly. 'We were here a week before we found it. It'll do, I tell you.' He took one of Sweet's bags and pushed it under the bench.

Alex was curious. He slid off the table and tiptoed

over to see what they were talking about. On his way he nudged a chair. It made a grating noise.

Both men spun around, startled. They stared at the chair.

Alex cocked his head. They looked at him but they didn't see him. They weren't mediums.

'Did that chair move?' whispered Sweet, feeling the hairs prickle up on the back of his neck.

'Nah. It's the wind,' said Sour with a slight trembling in his voice.

'This place spooks me,' Sweet swallowed nervously. 'OK, let's go.'

Sweet hid his two other bags under the bench and arranged some chairs in front of it. Satisfied, they left the orangery pulling the door shut and walking back in the direction of the hotel. They were still discussing the merits of their hiding place as they went. Alex waited till they were out of sight, then went to see what it was they were hiding.

He pulled a chair away and knelt down in front of the bags. He unzipped the first one and gasped. It was full of gold and silver. Goblets and rings and plates and spoons and daggers. He knew immediately whose it was: Etheldread's.

They had stolen Etheldread's treasure.

Chapter 14

Alex stared at the contents of the bags that Sweet and Sour had hidden under the bench in the orangery. Yesterday he had seen the big polished plate, silver and gold, with dancers and mythical beasts around the outside. Now he picked it up and held it. It was Etheldread's pride and joy. The one she polished every day. They must have found her tomb and plundered it.

He glimpsed his own reflection in the plate and the moon above him. He must find Etheldread. She must know what had happened. *And what if something had happened to her*, he wondered? He stumbled out of the orangery and ran down through the woods to the tomb in the cliff.

'Etheldread!' he called. Scrambling down a steep bank, he almost fell into the river, then he ran along to the bottom of the cliff.

The ivy had been pulled off the rock face and lay scattered around. A hole had been hacked into the stone door, the edges of which had been perfectly blended into the rock. The hole gaped like a dark mouth. It was big enough to climb through. The secret of Etheldread's tomb was out.

'Etheldread!' Alex called.

There was no answer. The trees shook in the wind. He went closer.

Tomb robbers! The very phrase sent shivers down ghosts' spines! He stepped over the tangled strands of ivy to the entrance of the tomb, and called again. Still, no answer. Alex ventured into the darkness. Then he stared in disbelief. The tomb had been wrecked. Rotten leather shields and armour lay strewn about. Several broken, rusty swords lay in a heap in a corner. Nearby, a crumbling scabbard, two thousand years old, lay trampled carelessly in the dirt. Alex picked his way to the dark end, fearful of what he might see. Only yesterday he had had tea here, surrounded by shining plates and goblets.

There was Etheldread's casket. At least that was still here. Alex blinked in the darkness, straining to see, then suddenly he froze: someone had pushed the heavy stone lid off the casket, and Etheldread's skeleton lay exposed. The bare white bones lay rigid and proud, arms crossed on the chest. Alex shivered. Had these robbers no shame? He tried to push the stone lid back in place – but it was too heavy. Etheldread herself – the ghost of Etheldread – was nowhere to be seen.

What would she feel when she saw this?

Alex stumbled back out of the tomb. Once outside, he ran up the path through the woods. He must find her. He tried to imagine her fury. What would she do? Tear Sweet and Sour limb from limb? Haunt them to death? Petrify them? And if they became ghosts? Surely she would torment them for eternity!

He came out of the woods and called her name. An owl sitting on a fence post watched him pass. *They can sense the supernatural*, he thought. Alex climbed the steps to the back lawn. It was empty – save for a couple of ghosts enjoying the night air. He studied the statues in the fountains – but she wasn't there. He looked into the walled garden but it was deserted, just the overgrown paths and foxgloves swaying in the wind. He looked in at the swimming pool – the usual gaggle of ghosts were lounging around, chatting and reading – but no Etheldread. He went on to the stable yard.

As he came around the back of the stables, Alex heard a curious noise.

'VROOM! VROOM!'

It was coming from the rusty wreck of an abandoned car. Someone was bouncing around in the driving seat. Alex went to investigate.

'VROOOOM! VROOOOOOOOOOOOOM!'

It was Castor, the coachman. He was sitting in the driving seat pretending to drive. His eyes were bulging, his face was contorted by a strange grin.

'VRRRROOOOOOM!'

'BOO!'

Alex popped up at the driver's window.

'Ahhhhhh! Errrrrrrrrrrrrrrr!'

Castor slammed on the brakes and spun the steering wheel. 'You made me crash!' he said accusingly.

Recognising Alex, he broke into a warm smile. 'Ah ha! You finished your holiday? Ready to go?'

'No. No,' Alex explained. 'I'm looking for Etheldread.'

'The one who rides a chariot? Her with all the war paint and the helmet and spear?'

Alex nodded. 'I have to find her – it's important.'

The coachman considered. He scratched his stubble.

'Ethel!' he yelled.

'What is it?' replied the warrior's voice and Alex saw the big ghostly figure put her head through the stable wall.

'Boy here wants to see you.'

'Etheldread!' he cried.

'Hello, scamp,' Etheldread stepped out fully

117

through the wall into the stable yard, with a shiver.

'Etheldread – your tomb – someone's been there and got in. They've taken your treasure.'

'They've what?' said Etheldread frowning.

'Two men. They've stolen your treasure.'

Etheldread's face darkened. Her eyes glinted angrily. Her muscles rippled.

'Show me,' she whispered murderously.

She scooped up Alex as if he were a baby and sat him on her shoulders – then off she went, taking giant, angry strides, across the cobbled stones. Castor had to run to keep up. They marched out of

the stable yard, past a couple of skeletons carrying bags of vegetables to the hotel kitchens. Then they turned away from the hotel, skirted the walled garden and plunged into the woods.

'I know where they've taken it,' Alex told them as branches whipped past his face. 'I saw them hide the bags in the orangery.'

Etheldread slowed. 'I want to see my tomb first,' she growled.

She marched through the undergrowth, striding over fallen logs and ignoring bushes and brambles. Alex ducked out of the way of overhanging branches

but leaves brushed his face. Soon they were at the top of a gully and Etheldread swung deftly down, grabbing hold of trees that grew out of the side as she went. In no time they were at the bottom by the river. Then she clambered over the mossy rocks to the steep part of the cliff, where the tomb lay.

When she saw the entrance, Etheldread picked Alex off her shoulders and set him on the ground.

'Ohhhhh!' she sobbed and beat her helmet with both hands. 'My Tomb! My treasure! My home.' She walked towards the hole that had been smashed into the cliff face. She touched its rough edges in disbelief. 'Romans!' she swore and ducked inside.

Alex looked nervously at Castor. Castor returned the look with a little twitch of his eyebrows. *What would she do now?* they both wondered. Would the great warrior Etheldread arise – and if she did, what terrible chaos would follow? They stared at the cave entrance, in consternation.

'Bad business,' whispered Castor.

Suddenly a dreadful howl came from within, echoing off the walls of the cave and amplifying Etheldread's anguish.

'My casket!' she bawled. 'They've opened my casket, laid bare my bones! Ohhh! I'm looking at my skeleton! My own skeleton!'

There was a clang and a clash from within the tomb. Castor took a step back pulling Alex with him.

'I think she's a bit upset,' he said.

Together they listened to the warrior bellowing like a bull in a rage. Etheldread smote the walls, she kicked the ground, she vented her fury to the very earth. Bits and pieces flew out of the entrance. A sword hilt, a rock, a bag of biscuits.

'Look out!' cried Alex as a metal shoulder guard flew past.

Etheldread's face appeared. She was past being upset — now she was livid with anger.

'I'll get 'em!' she declared, flexing her muscles like an Olympic weightlifter. 'I'll tie their legs round their necks and strangulate them!'

Castor coughed uneasily. 'Steady on Ethel. Don't be so passionate. Passion will cloud your thinking.'

'Don't tell me what to do,' she snapped.

'Quite, I wouldn't dream of it,' agreed Castor, retreating.

'He's right,' said Alex daringly. 'We should just — you know — stay cool.'

'Don't do nothing in a hurry,' Castor urged. He stepped defensively behind Alex. 'We'll get the robbers and then we've all their life to torment them. It's funny for me to say it but . . . there's no need to be hasty. Is there?'

Etheldread turned red in the face. She spluttered with indignation and the effort to control herself. Alex and Castor quailed before her. Then Etheldread did a strange thing. She walked over to a big beech tree and still shaking, wrapped her arms around it and hugged it. She hugged it with all her might.

Alex thought she was going to uproot it. Visions of Etheldread charging back to the hotel brandishing a vast beech like a battering ram, came to him . . . but she didn't uproot it. Instead she hugged it as if she were drawing energy from it.

When she turned back she was calm.

Only her lip quivered as she said, almost meekly: 'It's been safe for two thousand years – now it's stolen. I died two thousand years ago for that treasure! I'll die again if necessary.'

'Umhum. Absolutely,' agreed Castor. He took her hand gingerly. 'And seeing that we know where the treasure is – thanks to our clever young detective here – shall we just go and retrieve it?'

'Lead on,' said Etheldread. She stole a glance back to her ransacked tomb. 'It was my home,' she said piteously.

Alex led the way, past the boathouse and up the path through the other side of the woods. Etheldread followed and Castor brought up the rear with little comments about the speed of the clouds up there in the sky tonight, and the speed of the wind in the trees wondering which was faster, and why. The others weren't interested.

At the end of the woods, they passed through a small gate to the garden by the orangery. 'It's in here,' Alex said confidently. There was no sign of Sweet and Sour. Moonlight and silvery clouds were reflected in the glass of the orangery. Alex pushed open the door and pointed to the bench under the window.

But as his finger went out, he realised with a shock that under the bench was an empty space. Etheldread and Castor were looking at him oddly.

'But – they were there,' he told them searching around wildly. 'I swear Sweet and Sour hid the bags of treasure there.'

'They've moved them,' said Etheldread darkly.

They looked all over the orangery, under the benches and the stacked up chairs and tables, and round the outside too. The wind shook the trees. Vines scraped and tapped on the windows like bony fingers. After they had searched for a few minutes, they met again at the front. The treasure had gone.

Etheldread stroked the hilt of a dagger stuck in her belt. She was looking at Alex, the angry look back in her eyes. 'It's all right. I believe you, scamp,' she said. 'They had my treasure and now they've moved it.' She took out her dagger and turned it in the moonlight.

'We don't kill them until we've got the treasure back,' she declared and spat on the shining blade.

Chapter 15

Claire woke up early as usual, remembering with pleasure that she was staying in a hotel with her granny. She was vaguely troubled by a dream from last night, but it was only when she began to climb out of bed and found she was wearing her green coat *in bed*, that the events of the night suddenly flooded back to her.

Had a ghost really come into her room? She looked around for him. There was nothing, no sign at all. Had she imagined it? Outside, the sun was shining and a light wind shook the trees making the overgrown roses quiver and sway. She dressed slowly, as the details of Alex's conversation came back to her. She noticed the chocolate bar where he had left it on the arm of the chair; she could remember him walking through the bed. Then she saw a note. it read:

> **Please come to the**
> **walled garden at 3p.m.**
> **Just me.**
>
> **Alex.**

That was him. The ghostboy. She put the note in the pocket of her jeans.

It was still so early that she left Granny sleeping, dressed and went downstairs. The world felt like a different place. She glanced behind her. Were ghosts sitting on those chairs? Were they milling around the reception? Would she see them if they were?

The dining room looked empty – but last night it was full, packed like a school dining hall. Where had the ghosts gone? Or were they still there, invisible in the daylight? She sat down at a table by the window and looked out on the yellowing grass on the lawn. This was the window she had looked through last night . . .

'Are they serving yet?' a man had come in and now called over. It was Mr Sour. He was with Mr Sweet. They looked around. The tables were laid.

'I don't know,' Claire replied. 'I've only just come in.' Her voice trailed away. Behind the men she saw a tall white figure, in an iron helmet. It seemed to float above them, as if about to strike them down. Claire's eyes grew wide with astonishment.

A ghost – she was seeing another ghost. An ancient warrior by the looks of it.

'All day breakfasts!' complained Mr Sour with a sneer. 'I reckon seven o'clock is day, don't you?'

Mr Sour clearly couldn't see what was behind him.

'Unless it's seven p.m.,' said Mr Sweet lifting the lids of the empty dishes on the hot plate.

Claire watched open-mouthed. The men came further into the dining room. Two more ghosts followed: a caped man and a boy.

The boy! Alex – from last night!

Claire started forward when she saw Alex, but he held up his hand. He gestured her to stay away. He wanted her to ignore him. And she tried – but she couldn't help looking.

Sweet and Sour found the cereal and fruit juice and were served by a waitress. The three ghosts sat down with them and watched and waited as the men ate. Whenever Claire glanced over, she was struck by the angry faces of the ghosts. There were no jokes this time. She didn't like Sweet and Sour, but she couldn't help feeling that they were in danger.

Other guests now came into the dining room, but they didn't see the ghosts either. They walked past relaxed and concentrating on breakfast or their newspapers. *If they could see them*, Claire thought, *they would jump out of their skins and run a mile.* She remembered the word Alex had used to explain her ability to see ghosts: medium. She was a medium. It was something that made her feel special, but uneasy too.

All through the morning Alex, Etheldread and Castor the coachman followed the two men. They went from the dining room to their bedroom, from their bedroom to the grounds.

Claire watched whenever she could, but her granny soon appeared and suggested that after breakfast they go and sit in the sun, so Claire was obliged to be with her. She sat with her book looking across the valley to the hills beyond and every now and then caught sight of Sweet and Sour, who were walking round the hotel grounds followed by the three ghosts.

The ghosts looked like a faint milky-white light. They were hard to see in the sunlight and sometimes disappeared altogether, so Claire would squint at them, but sometimes would catch only the faint outline of a cloak or an arm or the side of a face.

The men seemed to be discussing something. A trip to London, their relatives there. Etheldread was smouldering with anger. Why weren't they going to fetch her treasure? It was hidden somewhere in the hotel, she was sure of it.

'If they've stuffed it down the loo, I'll stuff them

after it,' she grumbled.

'There's too much,' Castor told her quietly.

'If they've stuffed it in a chest, I'll stuff them in.'

Suddenly the men talked about the treasure:

'What'll we do if we can't sell it?' asked Mr Sweet as they sat in the sun on a wall. 'It's so old and beautiful,' he said.

The ghosts immediately gathered round to listen.

'Sell it?' mocked Sour. He looked over his dark glasses. 'You've got to be barmy! First − I don't know anyone who'd buy it. And second − the police would be on to us straight away. Sweet − you crack me up, you do − haven't you realised? We're going to melt it down and sell it in ingots.'

'What's ingots?'

'They're blocks, you blockhead. Like big bars of chocolate − only they're made of gold or silver.'

'Ohhhhhhh!' screamed Etheldread. (Claire looked up from her book.) 'They're going to melt my treasure down! The brutes! I'll kill them. I'll melt the rascals myself! I'll mash *them* into ingots.'

'Control yourself,' Castor urged. 'Don't kill them until we know where the treasure is.'

Etheldread bristled. 'I'll stick 'em in the gizzard,' she muttered under her breath prowling round the two men. 'I'll boil 'em in a pot,' she hissed.

'Steady on,' whispered Castor. 'This is the twenty-first century.'

'I am an old ghost,' Etheldread reminded him. She reared up theatrically. 'And I come from a violent time. A couple of thieves in the pot is nothing.'

The men returned to their rooms. The three ghosts trudged behind. Etheldread was running out of patience. While the men had lunch in their room and watched TV, she went outside to hug a tree and calm down. When she returned, the men were asleep.

'Sleep!' wailed Etheldread. 'How long can this go on? Eat, sleep, watch TV? We'll be here for a century. Let's just frighten them into telling us where the treasure is and have done with it.'

'We have to wait till it's dark,' Castor reminded her. 'We're too weak to appear in daylight. They'd laugh at us.'

'How about we get some snakes or something and put them in their bed?' suggested Alex. 'Or poison them? Or tickle them?'

'Bad boy,' said Castor, grinning.

'Not my style,' said Etheldread shaking her head. 'I want to fight! I'm going to fight them to the death!'

Meanwhile, in the crumbling walled garden, Claire sat on a bench. It was warm out of the wind and peaceful. This was a place that had once been lovingly cared for, but had fallen into ruin. Peach and apple trees grew wild on the south-facing wall. A greenhouse with broken glass had a bird's nest near the top of an empty iron frame. A garden shed with a sunken roof lay shut up, with earthenware pots stacked in rows outside.

There is nothing like the deep peace of a walled garden, she thought.

Suddenly Alex was there. He had been running.

'Claire.' He stood a little way off, in the shadow of a beech tree. He had left Etheldread and Castor. They were watching TV with Sweet and Sour.

Alex studied the human girl. She was wearing jeans and pink trainers and a T-shirt that had a picture of a giraffe and the word: 'Dude'. *Weird clothes — really bright. Twenty-first century all right*, he thought.

'Hi Alex,' she said and smiled tentatively.

Alex felt a tingle of excitement again. His senses seemed to come alive. He could smell grass and earth on a warm summer afternoon and it made him feel dizzy.

'What are you doing following those men around?'

Claire came slowly towards him, still unsure about what to do when you talked to a ghost. 'My granny thinks they're weird – and she hasn't seen you lot!'

'They are bad men,' said Alex. He sat against the tree and explained how Sweet and Sour had stolen Etheldread's treasure and how they were going to melt it down. 'Big things are going to happen. Big things,' he said.

'Why don't you go to the police?'

'We can't! What Sweet and Sour have done is not a crime – not in your human world. They've found some treasure. That's allowed. They haven't actually melted it down. And once they do, it is too late.'

'Can I help?' asked Claire.

'I'm not sure. Maybe.' Alex watched a butterfly flutter past. 'We just need to find out where they've hidden the treasure.'

'Why don't you appear before them? They'd tell you soon enough,' Claire told him.

'It doesn't always work,' said Alex, thinking of Grandpa's experience with the woman in the Indian Room at Halibut Hall.

'If only they could see what I saw last night, they'd soon tell you,' said Claire, remembering the terrifying hoards of ghosts in the dining room.

Alex looked up at her. His eyes narrowed. 'Thanks. You've just given me an idea,' he said.

Chapter 16

The clocks struck twelve. Midnight. Throughout the hotel the ghosts stirred.

One clock struck thirteen.

The ghosts sat upright, startled awake. Thirteen strikes was an alarm call. Something was wrong. They jumped out of bed and dressed quickly. Was a friendly ghost in trouble, did someone mean them harm?

Or was the clock broken?

Grandpa's first action was to wake Alex. He pulled back the covers and found a pillow. The boy had gone. The bed was empty.

Grandpa frowned. *What was the boy up to?* he

wondered. He'd been acting strangely since they'd come on holiday. *Mind you*, he told himself, (thinking of Miss Gibbons), *so have I* . . .

He sighed, smoothed his hair and slipped on his shiny, worn butler's coat. He was just checking his cravat in the mirror when the door burst open and Alex rushed in.

'Grandpa,' he panted, 'you've got to help.'

'Calm yourself, Alex,' said Grandpa sternly, then checked himself. 'Now, what is going on?' he asked more kindly.

'The men – they're packing their bags, moving out.' It took several minutes to explain all that had been going on.

Grandpa drummed his fingers together. He coughed: 'Aaaaaahem!' – a cough that said: 'Something must be done, and done quickly.'

Then Alex told Grandpa his idea.

They went downstairs. The ghosts were gathering in the library. Dr Jempson was calming them and at the same time asking questions. 'What's going on? Who struck thirteen? Be calm! Patience! Anyone know what's happening?'

Alex and Grandpa entered. Before Alex realised it

he was standing on a table next to Grandpa, in front of all the ghosts.

Grandpa cleared his throat,

'AAAAAHEM!' It was the cough of a leader. A 'listen to me' cough.

Alex noticed Grandpa's hands trembling.

'Go on, Grandpa,' he urged.

'My friends,' Grandpa began. 'This day has seen a terrible crime take place in the grounds of this hotel. Under our very eyes!'

There were mumbles and murmurings.

'A tomb – a tomb of an ancient Briton and fellow ghost – has been robbed!'

A grumble ran around the room. Etheldread slipped in through the French windows at the back. Grandpa warmed to his theme.

'Even as I speak, two humans are planning to melt down the rare and fabulous Roman treasure, kept for two thousand years in that tomb. The Moonbalm Treasure . . .' (Here Dr Jempson lit up with pleasure.) '. . . is of inestimable value. There are plates and goblets, jugs, necklaces, er . . . bottle tops, teapots, combs. Beautiful, irreplaceable treasure. Should we let this be lost? Should we allow it to fall into the hands of criminals?'

There were cries of 'No!', 'Never!' and even 'Over my dead body!' Grandpa puffed himself up, looking more like an old grey heron than ever.

'I am asking you to help us. Our plan,' (he put an arm round Alexander's shoulder) '*Alexander's* plan — is to frighten these humans, to terrify them into returning the treasure. And we shall use our keenest weapon. We are proposing a *mass apparition*!'

A ripple of excitement ran around the room. A mass apparition – that was a new idea.

'Are you with me?' cried Grandpa.

'Yes!' they shouted back.

'A hundred times!' cried Miss Gibbons proudly.

'Ghost power!' shouted Etheldread holding aloft her clenched fist.

Sweet and Sour had finished watching the TV in their room. It was past midnight. They were troubled by a curious wind that kept opening the door. A gong sounded and they left the room and walked into the hall . . . walked they − weren't − sure − why − down the stairs.

Halfway down, they stopped dead in their tracks.

A crowd of figures deathly white were pointing at them. A crowd of people from the past: fishwives and chimney sweeps, skeletons, soldiers and sailors, foppish gentlemen and elderly ladies, men in armour, men in their swimming trunks, miners, women in nightgowns, in tennis clothes. Strangled, drowned, squashed, diseased, all cried together,

The humans reeled backwards. Mr Sweet shrieked. Mr Sour screamed and ran in circles. Together they stumbled back to their room.

Immediately the ghosts broke into howls of laughter and began slapping each other on the back.

'It's cursed!' cried Sweet, hopping up and down in the bedroom.

'Let's go,' said Sour, grabbing his coat and putting it on upside down.

'The curse of the Roman Treasure,' cried Sweet, running on the spot.

Etheldread appeared through the door, shining with a green and ghostly light.

'WAHHH!' shrieked Sweet and ran into the cupboard.

'Oh, oh, oh, oh, oh!' wailed Sour. He ducked behind the curtain and tried to make himself as small as a mouse.

'BOO!' Etheldread boomed.

Sweet and Sour bolted to the bathroom and frantically locked the door.

Etheldread laughed, 'Huuuuuu-huuuuu-haaaaa.'

She seized the two daggers stuck in her belt. She juggled with them, spat on them, twirled them like drumsticks and prepared to lunge. Her eyes blazed with fury. Now Alex and Castor ran into the room, also shining with light.

'Don't kill them yet. Wait until they've told us where the treasure is,' Alex shouted to Etheldread.

'Come out,' Etheldread demanded, her voice trembling.

She strode through the bathroom door – mere locks would not hold her – but the men had gone!

The window was open. Etheldread looked out. Sweet and Sour were sliding down the drainpipe.

Etheldread grabbed the drainpipe and shook it, but it came away in her hand, and Sweet and Sour reached the bottom and ran.

Alex and Castor heard the roar of a car engine, then a scrunching and spraying of gravel. As they looked out, they saw a small blue car spin around and tear away, zigzagging crazily down the drive.

Etheldread cursed: an ancient Briton's curse, to the moon and the stars and the sun.

The car sped around the fountain, and as it did so the boot flew open and Alex glimpsed inside. Luggage. The bags of treasure.

'I know where it is. I know where it is!' he cried.

Castor and Etheldread looked at him.

'The treasure is in the car.'

Chapter 17

Behind them other ghosts were cramming into the bathroom, eager to know what was happening. Soon some sixty or so were jammed in there like commuters on a train.

'They got away,' explained Etheldread hollowly. She looked deflated. 'The treasure's in the car.'

'After them,' shouted Grandpa, his fighting spirit still alive.

'How?' said the cowman. 'We ain't got cars.'

'You're a coachman,' said Grandpa to Castor. 'Saddle up the horses! *"Castor None Faster!"* Remember? We can do it!'

All eyes swung to the caped figure of the

daredevil coachman. He looked uncomfortable. The ghosts' hopes began to sink.

'Castor is fast,' agreed Castor. 'But cars . . . are faster. It was just a bit of advertising, really,' he said, looking embarrassed. 'And anyway, we haven't got a car.'

As he spoke, a notion was forming in Alex's head. 'I can get a car – well, not exactly a car – a bus,' he said.

'A bus?' said a ghost.

'An omnibus?' muttered another.

Now all the eyes swivelled round to Alex.

He swallowed. 'I know a human,' he told them. 'She's a medium and she's a friend and we've been talking, and she came in that bus – the coach . . . she might be able to help, if . . .'

'You what?' asked Grandpa aghast. Dr Jempson fainted.

'Never mind!' cried Castor. 'Get the keys. We need the keys! Go Alex, go fast – there's not a minute to lose.'

Alex went straight to Claire's room. He went in alone. He called to her to wake up, then he explained that Sweet and Sour had escaped with the treasure in a car.

'I'm sorry,' she said sleepily.

'You don't understand. We need the bus. Where are the keys to the bus?'

'You can't take that,' Claire said sitting up in alarm. 'That's Granny's business. She's a coach driver.'

'But we *have* to have it,' Alex pleaded.

'But you can't drive.'

'Yes, we can. Castor can, he's a very good driver. Very good. Excellent. Please.'

Claire thought. Sometimes if you didn't do things immediately, you never got the chance again. 'Only if I can come,' she said suddenly.

Alex hesitated. The seconds ticked away.

What would the other ghosts say?

Who cared what they thought?

'OK,' he said.

Claire dressed as fast as she could and slipped through to Granny's room. Granny was snoring lightly. Claire tiptoed to the dressing table and found the keys. Then she went back to Alex.

'I've got to go with the coach,' she said holding the keys tightly to her chest. 'I've got to look after it.'

'OK – I said it would be OK,' said Alex. 'There are lots of ghosts out there,' he warned indicating the other side of the door on the landing, 'but they mean you no harm. Are you sure you want to go with us?'

Claire nodded. She felt nervous, but excited. Together they tiptoed back past Granny and into the hall.

The ghosts were there. They swooned and backed away when they saw Claire, seeming to slide together for comfort. She held Alex's hand – it was like holding mist, there was no warmth and no substance. The other ghosts were dimmer than Alex, but she saw them clearly enough, some were floating and hovering near the hall entrance. White, transparent, agitated figures. And she could hear their breathing – a gentle hissing noise.

'Hello,' she said softly, fearfully, to the group before her.

'*UMMMMMUMMMHUMMMMBUMMMMNUMMFF FFFFFFSSSSSSSSSSSS.*' the ghosts mumbled.

'Do you have the keys?' asked an excited figure in a cape.

'Yes,' she told him. 'But I am coming too.'

Castor looked at Alex.

'I agreed,' Alex told him.

Claire dropped the keys into Castor's trembling hands.

'Yeeeeeeessssss!' he cried and then they ran, swirling down the stairs, through the hall, out to the front. The ghosts following, gabbling like a herd of excited geese.

Castor unlocked the door to the bus and the ghosts piled in. Now they were like badly behaved schoolchildren, pushing their way on and arguing over who was to sit next to whom.

Some of them stared at Claire as they passed, but others seemed more interested in the adventure of getting into the bus, bouncing on the seats and examining the upholstery and seat pockets. Claire climbed in and a ghost kindly showed her to a front seat with Alex and Etheldread. Grandpa and Miss Gibbons sat nearby, Grandpa urging everybody to hurry. Crinkle the clown couldn't get his feet in, so he had to hang them out of the window. In the end about forty ghosts squeezed in.

Castor closed the door and started the engine. The ghosts abruptly stopped arguing and paid attention. In the driver's seat Castor was breathing hard. Something seemed to have come over him . . . the urge to speed.

'YA-HA!' he hollered to everyone's astonishment.

The bus revved, backfired, headlights swept across the grounds, windscreen wipers swept across the windscreen, they jolted forward and suddenly, sweetly, they were off – fast – spraying gravel behind them – straight off the drive, bouncing down a bank, over the lawn, towards the river.

'Look out!' cried Grandpa, visions of their previous journey in the coach and horses returning.

The ghosts screamed, the bus lurched, and at the last minute when they thought they were heading for the river, it swerved, crashed through a gate into a field of cows, before streaking across it and bursting out on to a road.

'YA-HOOO!' cried Castor. He shot the gears,

spun the wheel, and put his foot down on the accelerator.

The ghosts screamed with delight and relief. This was fast, thrilling, mad, dangerous – like life itself! Indeed they felt they were almost living again. They felt dizzy with freedom and possibilities. This coach could take them anywhere – across the world, over the rainbow, to a million different places.

'There it is!' screamed Etheldread pointing with her dagger at the car in the distance and narrowly missing Castor's ear.

They were alongside it in three minutes. Castor hooted. The ghosts peered out of one side. Sixty ghoulish faces at the window.

'Mass apparition!' shouted Alex.

The ghosts tried. They summoned up all the energy they had left, dredged it up from their reserves, and faintly appeared, like the first glimmer of dawn.

Sweet and Sour glanced up at the bus.

'Oh, my ancient aunt,' swore Sweet. 'Look at that!' He swerved.

'Keep your eyes on the road,' Sour snapped. He leaned over and looked up. 'Holy headaches,' he breathed. 'That's a host of ghosts in a bus! They're after the treasure.'

'Give it to them,' wailed Mr Sweet.

'Keep going,' said Mr Sour, thinking. 'They might do us in here. Kill us in the lonely old countryside. I've seen the films. We've got to get to town. We've got to get home and melt this lot down quick.'

'London?'

'That's it. We'll go there. Lose them. Go on, put yer foot down, Sweet.'

Chapter 18

'I got them in my sights,' said Castor. 'Now what do we do?'

'We board 'em!' cried an old sailor.

'Don't be stupid,' said Miss Gibbons. 'These are motor vehicles, not ships. They can be jolly dangerous.'

'Ram 'em!' cried the cowman. 'Give 'em a good rutting!'

'It's my granny's bus!' Claire told him indignantly. 'We've already driven over a field – she is going to be furious when she finds out! We cannot possibly *ram* another car!'

'Absolutely, quite right,' agreed Grandpa. 'We

must think this through.'

'We could drive until their petrol runs out, then we have them surrounded,' suggested a skeleton.

'What if ours runs out first?' asked Etheldread.

'Just keep following,' suggested Alex. 'They've got to stop sometime.'

Castor settled to following the little blue car. They went down the windy country roads, past inns and country houses to bigger, faster roads and then they were on a motorway heading to London.

'Whoooooohoooo!' the ghosts whooped. No one had ever been on a motorway.

'Fast, innit?' said the cowman, grinning.

'We's gonna take off,' squeaked a man with a tall wig, holding on to the seat in front.

Castor was busy trying every available switch. Headlights, windscreen wipers, heaters, horn, radio.

'Hey! Get this!'

Suddenly rock music blasted through the coach. Drumbeats shook the windows, electric guitar snarled through the air.

'Ahhhhhh!' the ghosts shrieked and covered their ears and kicked their legs in the air. 'Turn it off! Shut it! Horrible noise! Pop attaaaaaaaaaack!'

Castor found the 'off' button.

'I liked that,' said Claire.

Alex's grandpa gave her a funny look.

'Disgraceful racket,' he said dismissively.

It was still the middle of the night, so there were few other cars on the road. The bus hogged the space behind the little blue car. When another car passed, the ghosts worried that the occupants would look up and see a bus with no driver. So Claire put Granny's coat on Castor. Now it looked as if a coat was driving the coach!

'Well it's the best I can do,' apologised Claire, and the ghosts laughed.

After an hour or so on the motorway, they approached a big orange glow: London. There were so many street lights that the air and sky for miles around was lit up. The ghosts became excited. This was a big adventure. Every new sight brought soft cooings of enjoyment and wonder.

But Sweet and Sour raced on, into the city. They tore down a main road with shops on either side. Grocers, supermarkets, ladies' fashions, bakers, butchers, cafés, pubs – the whole world was here. But it was still the middle of the night and though the shops were lit, the pavements were empty.

They flew round a roundabout and across a bridge, over a flyover.

'YA-HA!' cried Castor as the coach revved up and clipped the edge of the roundabout. A car horn blared.

They shot through an underpass. Speed cameras flashed at them.

Claire covered her eyes. 'What'll Granny say?' she wailed.

'Good grief, it's London!' exclaimed Grandpa to Miss Gibbons. 'I hardly recognised it! Where's all the smoke?'

'It was you mucky Victorians who filled it with smoke,' said a ghost in the seat behind him. 'There was no smoke in my time.' The man wore a tall wig and had rouge on his cheeks.

'No sewers in your time either,' replied Grandpa. 'I should think there was a proper Georgian stink in Fleet Street.'

They squared up to continue the argument but were interrupted by a cry from Castor, 'Where'd they go?'

'Right!' cried Crinkle.

'Left!' cried the cowman.

'There they are!' said Claire, pointing ahead. They

were the other side of a small park. 'Look – they're turning.'

'They're getting away,' cried Alex as the bus reached the turning. The ghosts called out in consternation. The small mews street was too narrow for the bus.

'We'll never get through there,' said Etheldread.

'I can,' Castor told her. He stopped the coach and prepared to reverse. 'I'll have to smash into the shop window to do it,' he giggled. 'Breathe in everybody!'

'No, you don't!' Claire cried, horrified.

'Quiet everyone,' Grandpa stood at the front of the coach. 'This mews is a stableyard full of carriages and whatnot. There's no need to go in. It's a dead end – they'll not get far in a car.'

'Dismount! All soldiers on foot!' cried Etheldread, seizing the bus door. She pulled it open with a mighty tug.

Now the ghosts piled out and ran in a big group into the mews. They immediately saw the blue car at the far end. Etheldread reached it first. She peeled open the boot as if it were a piece of fruit.

The boot was empty.

The ghosts swirled around Etheldread, whooping with excitement. But this turned to muttering and cursing when they saw the empty boot. They looked around at the mews. Curiously – after what Grandpa had said – there were no carriages and horses. Instead a row of houses, all neatly painted in jolly pinks and blues, lined the cobbled street. Each had window boxes and potted plants and pretty signs on the front. One had a lavatory pan full of geraniums.

'Extraordinary,' said Miss Gibbons pulling a handkerchief from her sleeve and holding it over her nose.

'Search the houses!' cried Grandpa.

The ghosts fanned out and each chose a house.

Then, taking a deep breath, they all stepped together through the front doors and into the houses. So it was that the residents of Orme Mews near Paddington suffered a fearful haunting. Cold air swept round their beds; doors opened and banged shut; vases were knocked over. Voices called and woke them up: *'Nothing here!'* and *'I'll never find anything in this mess'*, *'If they smelt my treasure, I shall pour the molten metal down their throats'* and *'Now this is what I call a comfy chair.'*

The residents hid beneath the sheets and trembled in their beds, and though they saw nothing, they felt the chill presence of the spirits . . .

The ghosts stepped back into the street. There was still no sign of Sweet and Sour.

'Well, sooner or later they must come back for their car,' said Miss Gibbons. The ghosts began examining the car for clues.

'They can't be far away,' Alex said to Claire. 'Those bags are heavy.' He was looking at a white door that led to someone's garden at the end of the mews. He had an idea. Claire had the same idea. She walked over and pushed the door gently. It swung open.

Behind lay a passage that led between the

buildings. The street lights stopped here and it was mysterious and dark. Unnoticed by the other ghosts, Claire and Alex walked gingerly down it. The door swung shut behind them.

After about fifteen paces, they were past the buildings and there was a wall on their right followed by steps down. Alex started down the steps and then stopped. There was a deep inky blackness stretching away in front of him.

Water.

The houses backed on to a canal.

As he turned to face Claire they both heard a cough, so shockingly close that they shrank back as if they were about to be discovered going somewhere they oughtn't to be.

Then a familiar voice said out loud, 'Look at it! Heh heh! Lovely jubbly! Make about ten thousand beautiful necklaces!'

That was followed by more laughter.

Alex looked over the wall. There was a narrowboat right beside them! Just out of sight. Alex went back up the steps and jumped the wall easily. He crept towards the little row of windows in the roof of the boat that shone like yellow lanterns in the night.

Behind him Claire hesitated. The wall had broken glass on the top and she wondered where to put her hands, but then she gasped when something caught her by the waist and lifted her. She looked down to see Etheldread smiling. She had seen the narrowboat.

'We got 'em!' Etheldread whispered in Claire's ear and lifted her effortlessly over the wall as if she were a doll, then dropped her gently on the other side.

Claire stood on a patch of grass that stretched down to the canal. She realised it was the garden of the end house. The house itself was dark.

Keeping low, Etheldread and Claire joined Alex at the edge of the lawn. They peered down through the windows of the moored narrowboat. Two of the four windows were open, to let air in on this warm summer's night. It looked cosy inside, and they could see spider plants and red sofas and a kettle boiling. Then they saw Mr Sour holding up a big golden platter.

'This weighs a tonne!' he chuckled. 'We'll have to cut it up before we can melt it down!' He put it down and took out a spoon from the bag at his feet. 'Let's start with this.'

Claire looked at Etheldread. A look of fury was

growing on her face. Her woad–stained jaw was set; her eyes bulged, her mouth open.

'Come on,' she hissed at Alex. She turned to Claire and gave her a comradely squeeze on the shoulder. 'Wait here, my dear.'

Then Etheldread got up and stepped carefully on to the narrowboat. Despite her size, the boat barely moved. Alex followed, jumping softly on to the deck. Then together they took a deep breath and stepped through the door into the cabin.

It was bigger than it looked from the outside. There were benches with cushions and a table and a kitchen area with a bar at the far end. It was all painted in bright reds and greens. The bags of treasure stood at the far end. Sweet and Sour stood either side of the counter.

Sweet held an acetylene blowtorch to the spoon and was watching it bend under the fierce heat of the little blue flame. They were giggling like naughty boys.

Alex and Etheldread looked at each other.

'Now – apparition!' whispered Alex. Etheldread nodded.

They tried. They strained. They searched inside themselves for the energy – but all they found was weakness and sogginess. They had nothing left. After a minute, all that had appeared was Etheldread's big toe and a row of teeth.

Sour glanced in their direction. He blinked and rubbed his eyes. 'Well – blow me if I isn't seeing things,' he said. 'I could have sworn – just then I saw a row of teeth smiling at me.'

Sweet looked over. 'That is a trick of the light,' he said. 'Revenge of the gnashers! Ha ha!' he joked. When he looked again, the teeth had gone. He never saw the toe.

'Caesar's socks!' swore Etheldread. Abandoning the apparition idea, she marched forward and grabbed the blow torch.

'Look out! That's dangerous! They're here!' cried Sweet as the torch assumed a life of its own and began to dance in front of his face. Sour snorted.

'Stop it, I tell you. Don't play games. We lost 'em. They . . .' Sour's words died on his lips when he saw the flame. He stepped back towards the cabin door. Sweet joined him, shaking. Their eyes watched the blowtorch take on a life of its own. It came through the air towards them. Slowly. Deliberately. That blue flame was hot. Really hot. Hot enough to melt metal. Hot enough to burn skin with the slightest touch. They stumbled backwards. One step, two steps. The flame was making them walk out of the cabin. The flame was possessed. They had to watch it. Their eyes were riveted to it. They fell over on to the deck. The flame jabbed at them closer, whirling, threatening, stabbing at them . . . They scrambled to their feet, took another step back and – suddenly they'd run out of deck and with a look of surprise they both toppled into the water with a splash.

'Help!' cried Sweet.

'Look out!' cried Sour.

A flowerpot flew towards them. Then a bucket and a pan and a broom and a cup and a rope and the engine cover all began raining down on them. Then from the bank a little girl hurled another flowerpot, and suddenly a cloud of gravel started peppering the canal. The two tomb robbers swam to the other side and once there, looked back quickly and ran away.

'Oh, my beauties,' whispered Etheldread now rummaging through her treasure inside the cabin. She lifted a big jug and hugged it, then kissed it. She tossed a bag at Alex and picked up the rest herself.

'Let's go, Alex,' she said.

The ghosts on the bank helped Etheldread with the bags of treasure across the lawn and back to the coach.

There everyone marvelled at it. Etheldread was close to tears. Miss Gibbons sighed. Grandpa preened himself and admired the workmanship knowledgeably. Alex showed Claire the goblet he had drunk out of and Claire told Etheldread that she had seen things like this on television and in books. Only Castor was unmoved. He was at the back studying the engine of the bus.

'Never mind treasure – *that* is beautiful, eh? Pipes and wires and oil and gaskets and exhausts. Oooooooooh,' he moaned.

He closed the cover, went back and started the bus. He couldn't wait to get back in the driving seat. He revved it up with pleasure.

'It'll be nice to have it all back in your tomb,' said Miss Gibbons to Etheldread as they bowled back along the motorway.

'Yes,' Etheldread smiled and stretched her long legs into the aisle of the coach. But as the sky lightened in the east, her smile faded and a troubled look came over her.

'What is the matter?' asked Alex.

'Where exactly *am* I going to keep it?' asked Etheldread. 'I can't keep it in my tomb. Everyone knows where my tomb is now.'

'Hide it,' said Alex.

'Where? In a hole?'

'Maybe. Or another cave. Or in the hotel cellar.'

'No,' said Etheldread. 'It needs to go somewhere safe. Somewhere it will be looked after.'

Chapter 19

They got back to Moonbalm Hall just as the sun was rising. The ghosts entered the hotel triumphantly, holding the pieces of treasure aloft. All those who had stayed behind clapped and cheered their entrance. Even Dr Jempson and the skeletons joined in.

Unfortunately the front of the bus was damaged. Castor had driven it so roughly that the bumper was bent, the headlights broken, and there was a big dent on the side.

Claire felt awful. 'We can't leave it like that! Granny will be furious.'

Castor studied the front, stroking his stubbly chin.

'Don't worry. If you can keep your Granny out of the way for the morning, I'll fix her,' he promised, giving the old bus a loving pat and a stroke.

Claire had no choice but to trust Castor. So she and all the other ghosts went to bed.

But it was a short night for Claire. She got up with Granny only a few hours later and she went, bleary-eyed, to breakfast. It was a beautiful day, and they decided to rest in the sun, reading. This was perfect for Claire, because it kept Granny away from the damaged bus.

'I'm not in the least surprised you're not sleeping,' Granny told Claire as they took their chairs in the sunshine. 'This is the noisiest hotel I have ever stayed in! Bumps, bangs, clatterings all night. The plumbing is atrocious! I swear that I heard the pipes laughing and clapping last night! At one point I thought that they were talking. Really, I mean it!'

'I believe you Granny – I really do,' replied Claire smiling to herself. If only, if only Granny knew.

At the end of the morning Claire left her granny reading and raced round to the front of the hotel.

There stood the bus, gleaming. Claire sighed, a huge sigh of relief.

Etheldread decided to hide her treasure in the grotto where the walls and ceiling were encrusted with shells. But now everyone knew about the treasure, and she had a constant line of ghosts outside asking to see it. Etheldread couldn't turn them away especially after all their help. So for the rest of the week, she was like a tour guide, unwrapping her valuables so the ghosts could see them. She grew tired of this, and not a little grumpy.

Alex was given permission by Dr Jempson to go anywhere he liked in the hotel. He went straight to the library, the billiard room, the games room, the swimming pool, the music room and the mud room. He found he didn't really want to go to any of them. He preferred to be with Claire and Castor and Etheldread outside. They were his friends now.

And Grandpa was happy too. He was enamoured with Miss Gibbons and they read poetry to each other in an overgrown temple near the river. They were a fine couple, everyone said so. All the ghosts marvelled in particular at Grandpa. *What an inspiration!* they thought. Alex almost fell over when Etheldread described Grandpa as 'your sparky old Grandpa'.

At the end of the week Etheldread sought out Claire and Alex. It was daytime so most ghosts were asleep; only Alex was up, playing a joke on a hotel guest, dropping a spider into his ear and leaving nit eggs on his moustache. He was showing off to Claire. Etheldread sat on the wall nearby.

'I know it sounds strange,' she announced with a new casualness, 'but I've decided: I don't want my treasure any more.'

'What?' Alex cried. He left the guest and came over. 'You mean we went to all that trouble for nothing?'

'No,' said Etheldread. 'When the treasure was kept in my tomb, I liked it. It was safe and hardly anyone knew about it. But now I'm bothered by everyone all the time. And I can't leave it because I feel responsible for it.'

'Well, it hasn't been melted down,' Claire pointed out. 'That's a good thing.'

'I think I'm going to throw it in the river!' Etheldread announced. The two children looked horrified. 'It's quite normal. Iceni do that to the things they value. Offer it up to the gods.'

'What?' Claire gasped.

'It's a cool idea,' said Alex.

'It's a bad idea,' said Claire. 'Your treasure is valuable. It's precious. You can't just chuck it in the river.'

'I won't just chuck it in,' said Etheldread. 'We'll have a ceremony. Speak to the gods. Sing Iceni songs. Then we'll chuck it in.'

'If you're going to get rid of it, why not put it in a museum?' Claire asked.

Etheldread thought. Alex leaned back against the warm stone.

'Well . . .' said Etheldread, slowly. 'What's a museum?'

'It's a place where humans keep precious things like treasure and old historical things.'

'And I won't have to keep showing it off?' asked Etheldread.

'No, someone else will show it off – and everyone can go and look. Humans, ghosts, everyone.'

'I like that idea,' Etheldread smiled. She wasn't one to dither. 'Let's do it,' she said.

So Claire composed a letter to her granny explaining that she had gone on a little expedition and Granny was not to worry . . . and in the night they slipped away.

The next day a small group arrived outside the British Museum in London. It was very early in the morning.

There were six of them – Claire, Alex, Etheldread, Castor, Grandpa and Miss Gibbons – but the guards saw only one little girl. One little girl and two huge suitcases on wheels. She bumped the suitcases up the steps to the grand doors of the museum.

'I would like to see the director of the museum,' she told the guard.

'Have you got an appointment?' asked the guard.

'No,' said the girl, 'but I have something that will interest him very much.'

'I'm sorry. If you don't have an appointment then you won't be able to see the director,' the guard informed her. 'And I shall have to look through those bags before you come in.'

The guard scratched himself. 'Excuse me, but I think I have – something – oh! – in my trousers! Ow! An insect, or a bee or . . .' Suddenly he began jumping around.

'Couldn't someone go and fetch the director?' asked Claire loudly.

The guard found he didn't have a bee in his trousers after all but something had been tickling him. There was the sound of scurrying feet, inside the museum.

'No, Miss, I'm afraid I can't fetch him!' the guard informed her, adjusting his clothes. 'The director is a very busy man.'

'Then I'll wait here,' said Claire.

The guard folded his arms and scowled.

A few moments later, the director of the museum

felt suddenly, strangely impelled to stand up. He marched out of his office. He strode through the galleries. He reached the front entrance. The guard was standing to attention. The director stopped in front of the little girl. He looked alarmed. It was almost as if someone was holding him there against his will!

'Oh – thank you for coming!' said Claire smiling.

'I – couldn't – help – myself,' faltered the director. He sat down abruptly on a nearby bench, looking more and more surprised.

'My name is Claire and I have some treasure,' Claire told him. 'I'd like to put it in the museum.'

The director smiled. 'Now Claire,' he said kindly (and as if she were five years old). 'This museum is filled with treasures from all over the world. We can only display things that are priceless. It is very unlikely that we will be able to put your treasure on display. It has to be extremely valuable and interesting. Nevertheless – let us see.'

Claire opened one of the cases. Silver plates and jugs and necklaces and goblets spilled on to the floor.

'Is this valuable and interesting?' she asked.

The director's eyes grew as wide as the silver

plates. He leaned forward and picked up a goblet. His breathing became fast and excited. 'It is . . . incredible. Roman. First century. Neronian . . .' he seemed at a loss.

'Move back now, move back,' ordered the guard to some tourists who were gathering around.

Claire opened the other suitcase. More treasure spilled on to the ground. More tourists arrived. They began taking photos.

The director fell on to his knees and began feverishly examining the jewellery and the beautiful jugs and containers. He gasped with astonishment, crooned with amazement and sang with delight.

'This is the most important discovery of Roman treasure in modern times! It is beautiful. I will most certainly put this in the museum,' he squealed.

To his surprise, it felt as if he was suddenly hugged by a tall, strong invisible woman and kissed on both cheeks.

He recovered from his excitement. 'Where is it from?' He looked up to Claire.

The tourists shook their heads, and shrugged their shoulders, looked at each other.

'The little girl? Where is she?' he asked.

The tourists looked around. The guard looked.

She had gone.

Two nights later Alex and Grandpa's holiday came to an end. It was sad but there were things to be done at Halibut Hall, and as Grandpa said, all holidays must end sometime. So they packed their bags and prepared to leave the hotel.

Claire came to say goodbye.

'I'm going to miss you,' said Alex. 'You've made me feel more alive than anything in one hundred and fifty years. Please will you come to see me at Halibut Hall?'

'Yes, I will,' she told him. 'Granny drives all over the country – so I'm sure we'll be able to drop in sometime.'

'It's open to the public from Thursdays to Sundays. So you don't have to be invited by Lord Halibut. Which is good – because he is terribly stuffy.' Alex told her. 'You'll find me in the attic room overlooking the laundry.'

'OK,' said Claire. 'I'll find you.' She knew she would too. Somehow. She took his hand, trying to touch him, but she couldn't feel anything. Just a chill in the air.

Grandpa wrote Miss Gibbons' address on a slip of paper and wrapped it in his handkerchief. 'I shall never lose it,' he promised. 'I shall write to you and I shall visit. I think Alexander is old enough to haunt Halibut Hall on his own.'

'That would be lovely,' said Miss Gibbons. 'Maybe we should meet up and visit the museum, one day?' she suggested.

Grandpa purred.

Etheldread wasn't very good at goodbyes. She gave Alex a dagger with a red ruby in the hilt. 'It is precious, little scamp,' she told him and began sniffing. 'And so are you.' She suddenly started weeping.

Then she gave him a great awkward warrior hug and kissed him goodbye.

'We have so many friends now,' Grandpa told Alex, looking out at the farewell party. 'We'll be able to have a holiday whenever we want. I can't tell you how young I feel. Holidays are a fantastic invention!'

Alex smiled and settled back in the coach. This was the Grandpa he loved and admired.

'YA-HA!' cried a voice above them, and a whip cracked.

The two ghosts held on tight.